Also by Megan Winkler

Transmissions from Dating Land
Wake of Darkness
Ruins of North Texas
(with Mike Winkler)

Revolution 2

by Megan Winkler

Revolution 2
© Copyright 2013 by Megan Winkler
All rights reserved.

Cover design by Megan Winkler
Cover image ©*Mathias Rosenthal – Fotolia.com*

Published by Brainy Babe Micro Publishing

Author's Note

I feel that I need to tell you, dear reader, that there is no prequel although there may be a sequel to this volume. There is no *Revolution 1.* However, I know that the title implies that it's about the second revolution in a series. In a way, it is. The first revolution it refers to is the American Revolution. Many of the ideals from that revolution show up as themes in this story.

Chapter 1
Bryn

The ground gave under my feet; the moist floor of the undisturbed wilderness softened my footfalls. The tall grass, damp with evening dew brushed against my legs and the damp chill in the air flooded my nose and smelled of a fresh night coming on.

I was free.

I was terrified, and I ran, but I couldn't outrun the droning in my head, reminding me just exactly what it was that I ran from:

"We are one," we would recite each day when I was in school. *"We contribute equally to the Society, as we are members within it. We behave for the better good of the Society. We share our opinions, only to contribute to the greater good, insofar as we do so with strict correctness in our mind. We work together, live together, and we are one. We are all for one and in our vast numbers, become one."*

I would later find out that some call it "brainwashing." They drilled their ideals into us with such force and consistency that we soon learned it to be the truth. We were taught that things were the way they were because it was better that way.

We were not always one Society, we were told. We were once a warring people. We were once individuals. We learned that this is not the true way of humankind. We must not think of ourselves, but of the greater good—of the Society first and foremost.

They—those who live beyond our society—call the lasting peace which we enjoy, the result of what they call "The Great Conspiracy." We were warned against those who spout this poisonous rhetoric: They are false historians and bear false witness against our way of life.

After the war, when we struggled to care for ourselves, The Government provided us with stability and it took care of us: healthcare first, never allowing us to have any more than our neighbors; everything utterly equal.

We subsequently received equal pay for equal work. Finally, our genders no longer meant a difference in the Society. Economic competition was eliminated next, contributing to our collective peace. Now we live in harmony; none of us are without, and none of us have more possessions than the rest. We dress in similar clothing, made of organic materials which we learned long ago are the healthiest for us. We drive similar, electrically-powered cars, the injunctions for which have improved the air quality five-fold since their invention decades ago. We all contribute the same amount of community service, to help the other citizens of the Society of which we belong. And we are told that we are happy—

As I ran, the low branches tugging at my shirtsleeves as if to draw me back, I envisioned the maps in my head from my geography class. The States of North America stretches along the Atlantic Ocean and reaches inland. The States were once called things like Florida, Georgia, Tennessee, Maryland, New York, Maine and Missouri. Now the regions were designated by district based on the old names, but there was no quantifiable difference between them beyond climate and geography. The States stretches to the Mississippi River.

West of that is the Wilderness. The northern part of the Wilderness, which stretches into a place called Canada and over to the Pacific Ocean. It is there that a people live who survive in the wild and in ways that we are taught are false, unclean, and unhealthy. The Coast is the portion of land so far westward that we have virtually no contact with the inhabitants whatsoever. We were not taught about them as much, but the conclusion can easily be drawn that they are a disgusting people.

In the south, in the area that once were the states of Louisiana, Texas, Oklahoma, and New Mexico, is now the region called Republic of Texas. There they subscribe to archaic laws and live by something called a Constitution under the ridiculous notion of representative government, something which we have learned was a contentious and fruitless institution which produced only arguments and conflict. We often wondered at the way they live in the Republic, how they get on and are productive in anyway whatsoever, while they argue about the best way to govern everything.

The States are so peaceful, turning all of those difficult decisions over to those who are better equipped than we are to make such choices for the Society.

We live in peace. We live in equality. We are happy.

Chapter 2

I hated it. So, I ran.

I ran until the air burned in my lungs and my legs threatened to buckle under my body. And then, I ran some more. I ran to a place we had been taught to avoid, a place where the Underground Railroad opened up to our world. It was named for something that happened centuries ago, though we weren't taught *what* it actually referred to. I knew I would have to fight my way through, but once there, they'd welcome me with open arms. Or so I hoped.

I didn't know what I would say, or if they would let me stay, but I knew I had to try. I had to break out of the Society that would drive me mad; the Society that was supposed to deal fairly with us, the Society that provided safety for us all.

The Society that betrayed *me*.

I had broken a law, and I had not been alone. I was with my fifth partner. He was with his third. More importantly we were not supposed to be involved with each other on a personal level beyond basic friendship. .

The Government understood that close interpersonal relationships were healthy for our minds and our bodies. Permanent relationships were forbidden, but so too were significant relationships outside of those pairings.

There were very few of us who would have balked at the idea; it was what we were taught from the time of our own childhood: strong romantic or sexual attachments were frivolous. Sacrifices for the common good in this way were no greater than the sacrifices that our ancestors had made in the Great Wars. It was simply the way things were, and therefore most of us never fell into the trap of love because we simply wouldn't have dreamt it was possible. It's one of the things that made Quillan and me consider the shape of things, how things operated in this Government of ours.

We'd been planning something—our escape. We also spent secret moments with one another, escaping reality. We had vaguely known each other in school, but became instant best friends as adults. Our relationship developed out of that history together. His partner, Isolt, was frigid, and mine, Eunike, was female, so we found no interest in our current pairings. It seemed to make sense that best friends could get along well beneath the sheets.

We also wanted out of our society: He had the plan and I had the desire and fortitude to leave. I was destined to become something that I didn't want to be, and he wanted the chance to choose his own path. That necessitated a break from our past and a reshaping of our future.

But someone had reported our rendezvous to the Agents. Quillan fought back when the agents came. He shouldn't have. When they came to arrest him, he displayed physical resistance to The Government. The Agents of The Government killed him. I watched it happen.

I watched him fall under their cruelty. I watched as the last breath whispered through his lips. I could have reached out and touched him; he had been so close. I wanted to help him and I struggled to fight back, but I could not. His body convulsed under the electric wand we called a Down Stick, and he collapsed, his body still writhing from the current. A drop of blood slowly seeped from one nostril and his eyes rolled back in his head. I pushed against the hands that held me but was powerless.

Do not move, Trainee Craw, the Guard whispered in my ear. Of course he knew who I was.

I understood in that moment that I couldn't continue to be a citizen of a society which advocated such violent actions by its Agents. I couldn't remain in a Society that condemned anything even verbally defiant in opposition to The Government. Their reach was limitless. If they had that kind of power over our minds and our will, then I would break free of it.

As I ran westward, the wind burned my cheeks and I laughed a hysterical little outburst at the thought of *my* cheeks. Was it actually possible that I would forever be able to refer to myself in the first person, to really and truly talk about *me*? My heart pounded against my ribs. The feeling of the blood coursing through my veins was as exhilarating as the prospect of my impending freedom, even if it was a painful freedom, for I was utterly alone.

We had first dreamed of a better place, and I thought that maybe, somehow, my running honored his memory. I also owed it to myself. I deserved better than an unjust authority that was endowed with the right to change the course of my life with a single dismissive decision.

I thought about the life I was running from, the one I was leaving behind. The Society I had been a member of was equal, balanced, and fair. The great trick though, was that while Society told you that everyone was equal, of course it wasn't true. Everyone was equal below a certain status, but ancient governments taught our Scholars that a Society couldn't function without an upper stratus of individuals—a ruling collective—to oversee.

Chapter 3

Two Weeks Earlier

I had toddled up and down the stark white halls of the palace as a baby. The walls had reflective acrylic overlays so thick that a person could see their two inch depth just by glancing at them sideways. My parents had summoned me to them. Their private conference room was at the other end of the palace, attached to the complex I regularly trained in. I was sweaty and exhausted from a full day of instruction, but when they called, I had to respond.

I was born to the ruling collective; an ancient man may have called it a royal family. I had a static, matched pair of "parents." It was they, together, who made the pivotal decisions that impacted Society. Some ancient civilizations were called monarchies, with a male and female as heads of state, their children following in their path. I was one of these children, the second eldest. My sister, Melisent, was due to become the next *Regina*, the next queen. My brother Pax—the eldest of us all—had fled home years before and was assumed to be dead. My two other sisters were merely children.

I pushed the door open. It felt almost liquid in it coldness. Light reflected off of the glossy surfaces in the room. Everything was stark white, sterile in its perfection. The round room seemed like a vacuum against the outside world. As the door closed behind me, the air pressure changed and it was completely silent. A Guard rapped his staff against the white floor tiles and the sound echoed throughout the chamber. All Guards in the palace carried a brass staff for ceremonial reasons; I never understood why.

"Bryn Craw!" he called into the empty room, announcing my arrival.

I stopped a few steps in front of him and folded my hands behind my back, waiting. It seemed that if my family had their way, my lot in life was to wait until I was commanded to do something. I breathed a sigh of relief knowing that this would not always be the case.

The room was round like the turrets of old castles, but it was flooded with light and screamed of modernity. There were doors in this room, leading to other corridors of the palace, but they were so streamlined with the surround walls that they appeared invisible, as if the room were one solid piece of reflective acrylic. UV filters on all of the skylights kept the sun from harming those within, but the light produced an awe-inspiring, heavenly glow that nearly burned the eyes. The luminous tile floor echoed with the footfalls of all who entered. The room had an unparalleled burning coldness to it. There was no other room in the palace quite like this one.

A rustle of fabric preceded the appearance of the Imperator and Regina, my father and mother. My parents wore white robes that covered their entire bodies. Their heads seemed as if they were floating in space. Behind them, Melisent ghosted into the room. She was tall, pale, and willowy. Melisent preferred wearing icy blue robes over her clothing, which gave her an even more haunting appearance. Her raven black hair—the envy of schoolgirls when we were growing up—was partially covered by the garment's cowl. If it were allowed to be free, it would have been as glossy in its darkness as the room was effulgent with light.

I stood out in obvious contrast as I waited in the center of the room, abrasive to the overall aesthetic in my black uniform. It fit tightly: black skintight pants tucked into heavy black boots that would deliver a rib-crushing impact to the chest of an enemy. My black zip-up jacket was closed over a red tank top that I liked practicing in. My long brown hair was braided down my back in a thick rope of hair and I hadn't even taken the time to spruce up before walking into the room. I grinned at the fact that I'd also forgotten to remove the Bowie knife from my belt before entering the room. Not that I had any interest in killing anyone there.

"Ah, Bryn!" my father said and opened his arms warmly, although he did not make a move to traverse the gap between us.

I bowed my head slightly. "Father," I acknowledged shortly, falling into a habitual formality.

"How is your training coming along?" he asked.

"It is satisfactory," I replied. "I am learning much."

"And what did you learn today?"

"Today I finished my final instruction in the ancient martial art, Capoeira," I replied.

He clapped his hands together and grinned at my sister. "You are progressing much quicker than anticipated. You will soon make an excellent Regina Guardian."

Melisent stared at me flatly as I dipped my head again. I only gave her a passing glance. She had always been darkly beautiful—not that we as members of society were ever supposed to notice what made us different from one another. She was the type of woman who, if she weren't gorgeous, wouldn't have been able to get away with half of the things she did. The fact that she was the heir apparent just meant that those swayed by beauty had to do what she said anyway. Somehow, my sister had always been the type to be able to stomp her foot, pout, and get her way. Men were regularly at her beck and call, but she had no real natural authority. She could demand, and she could connive, but she wasn't the type of woman who commanded respect. Instead, she motivated people by making enough noise that they just wanted her to shut up.

If my sister could be compared to a goddess, it could be said that I look like everyone else. I can pass strangers on the street and they have no inclination of who I am. Agents know who I am of course and Guards recognize me—that's their job. My brown hair and fair skin blends into the population around me, and I like it that way.

"May I ask, Father, why you have summoned me here?"

He smiled. "Of course," he replied. "In four weeks' time, we will have a grand reception in honor of your sister." At this, Melisent smirked. "You are to be in attendance as both her sister and her guardian. Is that understood?"

I didn't have to do the math to know that I would be missing the party. "Yes, Father," I replied and bowed my head again.

"I don't think I have to tell you," he continued, habitually wringing his hands, "that only the most important persons will be in attendance. Security will be elevated. It is a time for you to watch and employ your training. It is not a time for you to be noticed."

I dipped my head to the side. "Of course, Father," I replied. *I was to be seen, not heard.*

"Good," he replied, rocking back on his heels a bit. "How are you and the girl getting along?" he asked, inquiring about Eunike.

"We get on quite well, thank you."

He looked quickly at my sister. "I hear you get on much better than most," he pushed.

"I do not know what you mean," I replied.

He narrowed his eyes at me, giving me the same look Melisent had inherited from him. "Perhaps you are too close to one another, hmm?" He smiled at me, like he knew something I didn't, as if he were referring to a situation that had nothing to do with Eunike.

Looking back on it later, I wondered if he knew about my circumstance with Quillan at that moment.

He strummed his fingers together and watched me carefully, but I could have stood emotionless before him all day, in ways that he could not endure—I had been trained to balanced and cool. I would not let my feelings betray me and reveal the truth. So it wasn't surprising when he gave up first.

There were rumors that my father was crazy. Actually there were rumors that he wasn't my father at all, which may have been why Melisent was named heir over me. The word whispered in dark corners of forbidden rendezvous points was that my mother had an encounter that resulted in her pregnancy with me. The public always loves a scandal, and I'd never pushed the issue. It didn't matter to me if I was related to my harsh father and my sister who was practically his carbon copy. I didn't care if my only link to this family was my submissive mother who stood quietly behind my father and let Melisent run roughshod over her.

My father looked to Melisent, who smirked at me when she finally deigned to look my direction.

Society dictated equality. My sister was deemed the "most able" of the children, all rumors about infidelity aside. Perhaps her middle rank in birth order made her perfect for the role. I did not know why, and I did not care. She was brutal, impulsive, spoiled, and petty.

With any luck, I thought, *I will never see my cold-eyed sister again.*

She turned her head to the side as she looked at me. "You are dismissed," she said.

I bowed again, turned on a heel, and exited the room as quickly as I could. If only I had known what she had planned for me.

I pushed the door open without waiting for the Guard to do it. A wave of exhaustion swept over me. I hustled down the ice-white steps of the palace, sliding my dark glasses over my eyes to reduce the sun's glare. My transport was waiting for me. I slid into the car and pressed a button.

"Home," I said, and the engine silently started as I fell into a deep sleep.

Chapter 4

Present Day

I looked between the trees. The sun was starting to set. Perfect.

Run west to the white house with the blue light, Quillan had told me days before he died, as we laid on the same pillow in the dark. He was, quite literally, the man with the plan. I knew minimal details in case we were discovered. I was too high-profile for schemes.

My footfalls were as quiet as they could be, running through the yet to be cleared underbrush of the forest. I moved as quickly as possible, but also as quietly as possible.

My parents would not tolerate my absence long, and they surely knew what had happened between me and Quillan at very least. They kept a watchful eye on all of their children—living typical

Citizen lives because everything had to be fair—while they groomed Melisent to take my father's place.

Quillan's face haunted me. He was only a few years older than me, but you wouldn't have known it. I remembered the light freckles on the bridge of his nose that disappeared if he had neglected the Government-prescribed sun block regiment. I remembered his laugh; the laugh that I knew so well that I could pick it out of a crowd. He'd been dead for a day.

No, Bryn, I told myself, *don't remember now.*

I pushed faster through the trees. I was afraid that something even as soft as my respiration would give my location away. I kept as close to the ground as possible.

Stop, something told me.

My breath wanted to come panting out of my body, but I clamped my lips closed and pressed myself against a tree, obeying the little voice in my head. I had been thinking of Quillan's death so much that I hadn't realized what my instincts had: I was being followed. I gripped the tree at my back and felt the bark dig into my fingers as they clawed into it.

I could hear footsteps heading my direction. They had actually sent *humans* out after me. I rolled my eyes, frustrated at myself. I'd have to be more careful or they'd find me, and whoever else I came in contact with. You could trick the drones I had expected, but humans had instincts which meant I'd have to be more careful.

If captured, I was likely safe, though others wouldn't have been granted the same kind of leniency. I blinked into the settling dusk, trying to get my eyes to adjust to the ever-changing light, and I didn't dare breathe. I closed my eyes and listened, hoping that my all-brown outfit blended into the foliage well enough to conceal me from them.

One, two, three, four, I counted as the footsteps got closer.

I chanced a shallow breath through my nose, hoping that they would not hear me. They came closer, growing louder in their approach.

My heart pounded from the exertion of running for so long, and now it thumped against my ribcage for a new reason. I inhaled slowly and closed my eyes. When I opened them, I was calm; the adrenaline had slowed.

"Which way did she go?" a male figure asked. He was dressed all in black and carrying a Down Stick.

"We cannot tell," another answered, this one female. There was other movement in the woods behind them—too many for me to take out.

I had to be quiet and I had to wait.

The first one was in front of me, maybe ten yards away. He looked from left to right, releasing and retracting his telescoping Down Stick, an all-black, nearly indestructible electrically-charged stick that could shock a citizen into submission—if beating them didn't do it first. As the name implies, it puts its victims down, but it usually did not kill them.

"It's late," the female called. "We will put a missing citizen's report out for her."

"The Imperator and Regina will not be pleased." He walked to his left, over to the female. I watched him go, only my eyes shifting, unwilling to move my body even an inch. "Nor will her sister. Melisent had plans for her, I should think."

"Perhaps they should have kept a tighter rein on her," the female said.

"It is treason to speak of them in such a manner."

"Of course," she replied, bowing her head slightly under his authority.

He caressed her check. "It is alright," he said.

The female immediately grinned and took his hand, leading him away from me and back the way they had come. She was all coy smiles and fluttering eyelashes. The sight made me shudder, but I'd seen that kind of thing before. I listened, counting their footsteps until I couldn't hear them any longer.

I finally exhaled; the air almost felt like fire on the way out. My fingers ached from my grip on the tree and I slumped against its trunk, sinking down to the ground. I rubbed my hands together and looked around. I had never been trained to evade soldiers, but it came so naturally to me. I knew I had to press on.

I pulled my compass out of my pocket—a gift from Quillan–and looked at it as it spun and then settled in my hand. I had to turn to the right a little to head due west.

"Here we go," I whispered to myself, pushing off of the ground. I was more careful this time, in case others were out looking for me.

The trees towered overhead in a way that I wasn't used to. The city I had lived in kept trees to a minimum within its boundaries. That's how most cities were, I'd been told. Most had few trees, but were surrounded by forests, to help clean the air. It was not as if we needed the wood for furniture or anything like that. Scientists had long ago developed an organic polypropylene to construct chairs, tables, even homes.

Unlike in the cities, these trees were allowed to grow as tall as they wished; the Forest Rangers cleared the underbrush out every six months or so, and it looked—and felt—like they were overdue.

My shoes rubbed against the skin of my feet, and I felt blisters starting to form. I had never run in my boot for so far or for so long before. I ignored the discomfort.

The night started to settle just when I began to hear the sounds of nocturnal animals around me. I needed to find a place to wait out the night. I was exhausted and had too far to go before I would make it to the white house Quillan had spoken of.

The night was a strange combination of the loud and soft. The trees above me rustled in the wind and I could see patches of violet in the sky above. At the same time, various little sounds began to grow louder: frogs singing to one another, insects buzzing, an owl hooting in the distance.

"Where to go?" I asked myself. It seemed strange to not have someone to talk to, but I couldn't decide if I felt stranger talking to myself or keeping silent.

My eyes kept traveling up the trunks of trees, up the branches, and towards the sky. I laughed out loud at myself for not coming to the conclusion sooner.

"The trees," I said, and began looking for a nest to hole up in.

I needed to find a sycamore tree—I didn't have a clue how I knew that, but I knew it was the kind of tree suitable for camping in for the night. I looked for a thick trunk with peeling grey bark. I pulled a long, thick vine from out of the ground, it wasn't the poisonous kind, and carried it with me, stripping the leaves off as I walked.

Thankfully it didn't take long before I'd found what I was looking for and began climbing.

I clamored up into the limbs of the tree that reached toward the sky like an upturned palm. I settled against one that leaned toward the south so that the breeze gently blew in my face. Wrapping the vine around the limb twice, I then tied it around my waist so I wouldn't fall out of the tree if I fell asleep.

I leaned my head back against the limb and listened to leaves dancing in the wind like nature's wind chimes. I thought back to the tales of my brother, Pax, who had run away from home when I was still a little girl. I wondered if he'd come this way, if he'd been as inexplicably good at escaping as I was.

"Sycamore," I said to myself and picked at some of the shedding bark on another limb nearby.

It came off in a thin paper sheet, curled like a thin tube of bamboo but more fragile. I turned it over in my hand, feeling the rough outside surface and the smooth inside curl.

"How do I know what you are?" I asked the tree.

The only answer I received was the chatter of the leaves.

I sighed and watched one particular leaf dance in front of a star, hiding it and then revealing it over and over in a hypnotic fashion until eventually the leaf wasn't there anymore, and the stars were hidden and the world seemed black.

I was back in the room I'd shared with Quillan. There was a red glow to the room, which didn't seem right. We didn't have a red lamp. I walked toward the window—the glow seemed to be everywhere—but it felt like I was moving through water. Every gesture was labored and deliberate.

"Bryn," Quillan whispered. His voice was rough.

I turned around and saw him standing there with a bloody nose and his hair disheveled, as if he'd just picked himself up off the ground.

"You're dead," I whispered back.

"Doesn't matter," he replied.

"Why did you have to die?" I asked.

"Doesn't matter."

"I'm alone."

He smiled at me. "Doesn't matter."

He reached towards me and I reached for him, but our hands never met, no matter how hard we tried to grasp the other.

"You don't need me," he said, and I knew he was right. "You may want me, but you've never needed me."

Suddenly men dressed in black came running into the room. They shoved me out of the way and knocked me down. How did they move so quickly in this water-like space? I tried to push myself off of the ground, but it felt like my hands were sinking into the floor. They beat Quillan over the head again.

Why? Don't you know he's dead already? I wanted to yell but I couldn't get my mouth and my voice to cooperate.

The men in black dragged him out of the room while I struggled to stand up. Useless.

I became aware of something else then, of a cool caress on my cheek. Something was rough and scratchy beneath the other one.

28

Blinking, I realized that I was back in my tree and the sun was just beginning to crest over the horizon. I lifted my hands and looked at them. My fingernails had dug little crescent moon-shaped indentations into my palms. My arms felt weak, like I'd been fighting things in my sleep.

I untied the vine that had done its job well—I hadn't fallen out of the tree—and slid down the trunk slowly. I started walking again, looking for berries or something to eat.

"It's going to be a long day," I said to myself resolutely.

Chapter 5

I had been walking all day. I was hot and tired, but hopeful. I had to be close to the outpost-like location I expected to see soon, the last settled area of the world I was leaving behind.

Just as the sun was setting, I caught a glimpse of a suburban housing subdivision here at the edge of the States. I was almost into the wilderness beyond it. I knew I was at the right place. Now I had to find the white house with the blue light.

I exhaled as I took the sight in. The subdivision was made up of tenements that resembled what used to be called row-houses or townhouses. They were all connected, one with another, each with glittering solar panels on top that reflected the rising moonlight overhead.

And of course, they were all white.

Okay, I thought to myself, *blue light in the window.*

I could do this. I scanned the subdivision from the hill I stood upon. Although I could see just about every dwelling, but there were several homes that blocked the view of the windows for others. I had to get down there.

I slinked along the side of the hill and crept into the first street I could find. Curfew would have already begun for the night, so if I encountered anyone, they would have been breaking the law just like me. They could not tell on me without turning themselves in, and no one wanted to deal with the Agents' arbitrary punishments for such offenses. I felt reasonably safe, but I did not want to be sorry.

I slid along the length of one whitewashed wall; the veneered finish smooth against my back. I turned the corner and scanned the length of the street cautiously and saw nothing. Slipping across the street, I stood at another corner and looked down the lane, again seeing nothing and no one. Sighing, I moved to cross the next street, but something out of the corner of my eye caught my attention.

Was it? Yes! It was a faint blue tinge around a window. My heart raced. I backed against a wall and crept quietly along the row of houses until I finally made it. I looked around to make sure no one had followed me; that no one had stuck their head out the front door to catch the person they had seen sneaking by their windows. The street was empty, except for me.

I smiled to myself and looked at the window again. Sure enough, it was lighted blue. I wondered how they could get away with it, but colored light bulbs were popular–symbols of individuality permitted within the mandated parameters from The Government. Looking up the street, there were tints of purple, yellow, green, and orange in various windows here and there. I realized that with law-abiding citizens, there was little risk in lighting your window in code since no one ever went out at night.

Unless they were up to no good…

I stared at the front door, identical to its neighbors'. I was to scratch at the door, 'like a cat,' Quillan had said.

I shrugged and scratched at the door.

Mid-scratch, the door swung open. I was pulled inside in one swift motion.

"Were you followed?" the faceless male voice asked. It was pitch-black inside.

"No," I answered.

"Is it just *you*?"

"Yes, we...*I* am alone."

"Come on," the voice said, pulling me away from the front door and the very faint blue light in the window.

The building smelled like just like a home, full of food and laundry smells. Something very appetizing had been prepared not long before, I could tell. The ground felt plush underneath my feet, as if the floor springs that were standard issue in all houses were still very new, but I still couldn't see anything.

"Come this way," he commanded and I followed. "Watch your step."

He led me down a dark hallway—all of the lights were off.

"Be very careful now," he said. "The owners are out so we can't turn the lights on."

"Makes sense," I whispered and followed him down. Quillan had told me that we'd be using a house that would be empty; the owners were on vacation. Members of the Underground Railroad regularly donated their homes to the cause, but were never on location as a means of protecting themselves. If Agents found squatters in a vacant house, they would appear to be exactly that: trespassers of whom the owners had no knowledge.

The room was stocked with food packets, jugs of water, and various other survival supplies, as if the occupants had been preparing for a war.

"Here we are," he said, turning around so I could see him. "We'll be safe in here for tonight, and tomorrow we'll get a move on."

The youthful voice I'd heard in the darkness didn't match the creased face of the man before me. He was probably in his mid-sixties, with graying hair and bright green eyes. He was about my height, which made him a fairly short man. He was comfortably overweight, probably by only about fifteen pounds. He had a friendly face and his smile was infectious.

"Sounds good," I replied.

"Well," he said with a smile, "I'm Drest, and you are…?"

"Bryn."

"Good to meet you. How was the trip in?" he asked.

"It was alright. It wasn't the way I'd planned," I admitted.

"What do you mean?" he asked.

"I was supposed to come with my—" I hesitated, "friend."

He watched me carefully and I wondered what he was thinking.
What did this stranger think of me? I glanced around the room.

"Is that a *door*?" I asked incredulously, taking a step forward.
There was a small square of a trapped door in the floor. I knelt
down to look at it.

"Yes," he replied. "They really run the Underground Railroad
underground. At least part of the way, I'm told."

"Wow," I whispered, running my fingers over its edge.

He nodded. "So, I guess it's just you and me, kiddo."

I smiled. "I guess so."

I looked around the room. The space was sparse, with a couple of army-issue canvas cots arranged side-by-side. Overhead, bare light bulbs hung primitively from wires that came out of the ceiling. It was clearly a temporary shelter, but the floor was made from high gloss black tile and the reinforced walls were the same white acrylic I'd been accustomed to all of my life. Kitchen appliances sat in the corner, small in size but utterly modern, with voice-activated controls and self-cleaning features.

I scratched my arm, acutely aware that my entire body felt gritty— as if I'd just spent the day running through the wilderness.

"Where can I clean up?" I asked.

Drest point to an unassuming door in the corner. "Over there. There's a shower and everything." His eyes grazed over my face as he tried not to be obvious about the fact that, clearly, I was a mess.

"Thanks," I replied

The bathroom was completely finished out with the latest technology available back home. Lined in the same polypropylene that everything was built of back home, the room had a large shower, a toilet, sink and mirror, and most importantly, a lock on the door.

The light came on as I stepped inside, and pulling the door shut after me, I murmured, "Lock," and the door quickly acquiesced, the light on the knob turning green.

I sighed at the thought of hot water and the plush towels waiting for me. Looking around, I finally caught sight of reflection, and gasped.

My brown hair was matted and tangled, bits of leaves and tree bark woven into the locks. My green eyes were ringed with shadows and the whites were red from the stress. My face was streaked with dirt, and my clothes were caked with mud.

I groaned again at the realization that these were the only clothes I had.

"How wonderful," I grumbled sarcastically under my breath.

Shrugging out of the clothes anyway, I opened the shower door. I pushed a button to activate the water and pushed another to make it hot.

There were multi-directional heads in the small cube of a shower and the steam began to accumulate quickly. I sighed in exhaustion and stepped one foot into the heavy stream of water.

"Hey kiddo!" Drest called through the door.

"Yeah?" I called, pausing.

"I forgot to tell you there are fresh clothes in the linen closet. In case you want a new set," he called.

"That's great, thanks!" I called back.

"Sure thing," he called.

I smiled at the thought of fresh clothes and stepped into the shower. I just let the hot water rush over me.

I didn't think about the trek I'd just finished. I didn't think about my family or the Agents out looking for me. I didn't think about the rumbling in my stomach or the parched feeling in my throat. I leaned against the wall, letting the scalding water rush all around me, enveloping me, and I let the emotion finally come.

I let myself remember:

I imagined Quillan and me running through the forest. I pictured him here now—we'd probably be splashing each other with water. I remembered the times that we had broken curfew and sneaked off to sit out under the stars, or the times we'd run away to some secret location, when we'd talk in code and make our plans.

Just days ago I had been sure that we were going to get away with escaping together, that we had tricked the cameras and the retinal scanners that could read not only who you are, but your emotional state–checking for signs of dissention and signs of stress.

I had been lying beside him, in his bed—his partner had been away for work for the night. We had been exchanging jokes. I had thought vaguely of getting dressed and going home when they had suddenly burst in. Agents who seemed slightly familiar, had swarmed into the room like hornets.

I had jumped out of bed and lunged for one of them. He struck me on the head with his Down Stick and I fell to the ground. He wrapped something quickly around my wrists as four men rushed Quillan. I had kicked at the one who pushed down on my back with his knee.

One of the Agents began to drone on in the obligatory speech: "Quillan Noe and Bryn Craw, you are to cease and desist. You have acted against the balance of Society. For the greater good you are—"

In that moment I stopped listening. I had watched as Quillan kicked one man in the hip, sending him to the floor in a scream of agony—the hip was most likely broken. With his free arm, Quillan had struck another in the face and the third that had held him was soon kicked so hard in the stomach that he slumped against the wall behind.

"No!" I had yelled, seeing five more overtake him, while the Agent who had held me dug his knee painfully into my back. Another one stood threateningly over my head.

In the same instant, the largest Agent in the room took two strides towards Quillan and planted the Down Stick firmly on his head as he struggled to get free. His eyes locked with mine in a moment of terror, and his blood-curdling moan was suddenly cut off by his unconsciousness. He had seized uncontrollably in the Agents' arms, and they dropped him to the ground, the Stick still firmly on his head.

I froze in the grasps of the other Agent, when the leader turned to glare at me. His cold eyes had reminded me of someone at the time, and he sneered.

"Pick her up," he said.

Two other Agents helped my captor pull me up from the ground. One twisted my bound hands behind my back painfully. I looked at Quillan helplessly.

"Are you going to fight us?" he asked, finally releasing Quillan's body from the grip of the Stick.

"No," I had replied, staring down at Quillan, my breath huffing in my chest as I struggled to keep tears of anger from my eyes. I had wanted nothing more in that moment than to kill them all.

"Good," he replied and nodded to the others. "You will receive your new partner tomorrow."

The Agents who had held me unbound my hands and went to collect Quillan's limp body, silently removing him from the space.

My eyes froze in the spot where Quillan had lain, and I could not even blink. "We thank you," I answered, giving the customary reply Agents had come to expect in our twisted, horrible world.

They left without another word. I don't know how long I had remained where I stood, but soon the night faded into day. Time passed and I did not realize it. I simply stared at the white sterile floor where I'd last seen him.

That morning, appliances had begun to switch on, and the clicks and hums of the small machines were what finally broke me free of my seemingly comatose state. It was then that I grabbed my most non-descript outfit: brown pants and a brown shirt and headed for the door. I had taken nothing with me. I knew that the retinal scanners would already be picking up my anxiety when I passed one. A bag thrown over my shoulder would have been too suspicious a thing for Them to ignore.

I had left earlier than planned and I realized now in fact how lucky I had been.

***

The shower water started to run cold, bringing me back to the present—they must not have installed a continual water heater. I felt simultaneously exhausted and relieved that the brisk water pulled me out of that memory.

I spun around once to make sure the soap and shampoo had all been rinsed off of my body before pressing the button to turn the water off.

I wrapped a surprisingly fluffy towel around my body, stepped out of the shower, and walked to the closet. Hanging inside were several different articles of clothing, both for men and women. There was a black pair of pants in my size, and a steel blue shirt with long sleeves. I pulled both on, and just as my head emerged through the neck of the shirt, my eye caught a glimpse of something silver and reflective sitting by the sink.

Pulling the sleeves on, I reached out and grasped the small foil-like packet.

Permanent Hair Modifier.

I flipped it over, reading the brief directions and explanation. Apparently I could take the enclosed pill and my hair would be permanently changed in color and texture—at the genetic level, no less.

"Yeah, right," I mumbled to myself. There were always rumors of such things, but everyone knew they were fake—unless they actually weren't.

"Feel better?" Drest asked as I walked out of the steamy room, the packet still in my hand.

"Yes, thank you," I replied and then held the packet up for him to see. "Did you take one of these?"

He chuckled. "Yeah, she told me to."

"She?"

"Decima, the girl who was here when I showed up: She gave me instructions, showed me where everything was, and told me she'd be back tomorrow."

I nodded. "Are they supposed to work?"

He shrugged. "She said they did. Her hair was bright blonde and curly. She says it was dark brown and straight as a board before."

"Hmm," I mused and then thought, *Might as well.* I popped the capsule in my mouth and dry-swallowed it.

"We're supposed to wake up tomorrow morning with new hair," he explained with an amused shrug.

"Should be interesting," I murmured.

"Right," he agreed, and then held out a bowl. "I made some dinner. Would you like some?"

"Sure," I replied. "Thank you."

I took the bowl of proffered noodles and sat on one of the unoccupied cots. He had clearly chosen the one closest to the door, so I settled for the third one down, giving us both room to spread out.

"So why are you here?" he asked.

I shrugged. I really didn't want to talk about it. He did not wait for me to answer.

"Well, they were going to reassign me," he said softly.

I stopped chewing mid-bite and looked up. He stared off into the distance, seeing something that was not there.

"What do you mean?" I asked, but I thought I already knew.

"It was not time for Charis and I to be reassigned; we had a few more years together. When you get to be my age, they don't reassign you as often, but she got sick."

"What happened?" I whispered.

He shook his head. "The doctors said she died from natural causes, yet she had seemed so well just the day before. They tried to reassign me after she died, but—" he shrugged "—Charis was it for me." He said like it was a confession. He looked into my eyes. "I don't see anyone but her."

I dropped my eyes out of respect.

 "And you?"

"My friend and I planned to escape together," I answered. "Quillan and I weren't paired up; he was my best friend. He was killed," I replied. "I couldn't stop them."

"They killed him?" he repeated quietly.

"Yes," I answered. "After that, I knew that I couldn't live in that kind of society anymore. When the Agents found us, Quillan fought back. I was restrained."

He looked down at the bowl in his hands and shook his head remorsefully. "I've heard it happens. I am sorry."

"Yeah," I replied dismissively. "Me too. I couldn't stop them. That's the part that bugs me the most."

He shook his head again. "No, you couldn't have," he agreed. "There's nothing you could have done. They would have killed you."

I shrugged. "I don't know. Doesn't matter."

We were quiet for a time.

He sighed, and returned to musing about his partner. "Charis was always the adventuring type. She had such passion for life—like she hadn't been born here. I was glad we were assigned as mature Citizens. She made me laugh all the time. We explored everything together, at least everything The Government would let us explore—you know. I've been planning this for years—if she were the first to go." He looked up at the ceiling wistfully. "She may have been my greatest adventure, but I'm going to see if I can find one that comes in at a close second."

I couldn't help but smile. We were a pair: seeking freedom from the Society with the memory of someone else on our hearts.

He sighed and slapped his hands on his knees. "Well, I am going to sleep." He stood up and held his hand out for my bowl. "Are you going to eat that?"

I handed it to him. "Thanks, I'm done."

He nodded and offered me a smile as he took the bowl from me. I fell back onto my pillow and stared at the ceiling. It was lined with wide metal beams that formed the floor of the house above.

"See you in the morning," he said, lying on his own cot.

"Lights out," I called, and the lights obeyed.

It did not take me long to fall asleep. I saw the image of Quillan falling in a heap on the floor again, feeling a stab of remorse, but the regret dissipated quickly, diminished by my body's utter desperation for sleep. I soon was blissfully unaware of my new surroundings, Drest snoring softly two cots away.

Chapter 6

Present Day: Decima

Decima looked at the world upside down. The night had been one for camping in the wilderness and she had learned long ago that the best way to combat stiff muscles, aches and pains while sleeping under the stars was to practice yoga.

The sun had risen over the horizon as she watched – between her legs – the light had crested the mountains while she breathed through downward facing dog. Stepping forward, so that her feet met her hands, she let her body hang, feeling her back relax into the pull of gravity's gentle hands.

She slowly stood up, stretched her arms across her chest and walked further into the cave to retrieve her boots. Emerging from the cave a few moments later, a pack on her back, she exhaled happily. It was a good day.

She pulled herself up cliff faces and slid down slopes with an adventurous spirit that few people would have paralleled. That was why she'd been chosen as an ambassador of sorts – the kind of person who went to safe houses on the edge of the "civilized world" to escort refugees to Texas. There were supposed to be just three this time around; there were fewer people escaping these days.

Decima often wondered if it was because it was getting harder and harder to get out of the States or if the rumors were true. Word was that the younger generation had started to ask questions, had started to doubt The Great Conspiracy. Refugees brought back stories of underground meetings: dance halls, libraries, and salons – places where like-minded people could share ideas without the risk of arrest.

She hefted herself up to the top of a bluff and looked north. The rooftops of the nearby subdivision could be seen on the edge of the horizon. She had a few more hours to go, but it was now in sight. She shielded her eyes and looked at the sky above, her hand saluting the celestial realm. Her darkly tanned skin never burned, but the warmth felt nice. She was so used to being outside.

Smiling at some errant thought, she skipped forward and onward to the settlement, gleaming white and shining in the new morning sun.

Chapter 7

Present Day: Bryn

There must have been a window somewhere in the bunker-basement we'd spent the night in, because bright, natural light filtered into where I laid asleep. Its caress woke me up actually, as it filled the small underground space. I turned over to see that Drest had already stripped his own cot and was currently occupying the bathroom.

I rolled onto my back with a groan and rubbed my stiff, sore neck. The stretched canvas cot neglected to provide the support I was used to. At home, everyone had highly ergonomic mattresses, calibrated specifically for the sleeper or sleepers—it was the most healthful way to sleep. This temporary shelter held everything that was necessary for life, but lacked many of the comforts that I was accustomed to. The cots were a prime example. Their only benefits seemed to be that they kept sleepers off of the ground and they could be packed quickly and easily. Still, my unsupportive cot was better than roping myself into a tree in the hopes that I didn't fall out while sleeping.

"Good morning," Drest called from the doorway.

I turned my head to look at him and found myself smiling at the slightly wavy, quite red head of hair he now had. Gone was any trace of his grey locks, and he instantly looked ten years younger.

"Nice hair," I complimented.

"Ha!" he laughed good-naturedly. "You too."

I grasped my hair and felt the difference immediately. I pinched a shiny, jet black, straight lock in front of my eyes and looked up at Drest in surprise.

"Wow," I whispered, stumbling out of bed—if it could be called that—and pushing my way through the doorway.

"What do you think?" he asked, cautiously. He clearly knew what hair can mean to some women.

"I like it," I replied, staring wide-eyed at myself. "I like the change for both of us."

"I didn't expect it to be so drastic," he admitted, looking over my shoulder at his own reflection in the mirror.

I shook my head slowly at my reflection, locking eyes with his. "It makes you look younger," I supplied.

"Thanks," he answered. "Yours makes you look older."

"It makes me look like my sister," I replied with a frown. "I am going to cut it."

"Really?"

I nodded, rummaging around in the drawer for a pair of shears, sure that they would have left some in there for that reason. I smiled when my hand landed on a pair.

"I'll leave you to it," he said and backed away from the door.

I smiled and set to work, trimming the thick locks into a short, spiky frenzy. It stuck out in wild bunches, like a wind-blown daisy. When I was done, I sighed in satisfaction. I liked it.

"What do you think?" I asked, rushing into the room where Drest was waiting.

He laughed. "You look like a psychotic pixie."

"Really?" I couldn't help but smile mischievously. "How do you know I'm not?"

Suddenly, another door that I had not noticed in my short time there opened and in stepped a very tall, tan, and lean woman with a shock of white-blonde hair. Her eyes shifted so quickly from me, to Drest, and then back again that it made me wonder if she were really human.

"It's just you two?" she asked; her voice was clear, like a bell.

I nodded as Drest answered, "Yes."

She nodded back. "Okay."

The woman walked towards me with an authority that I'd seen in few people. Clearly, she had no clue who I was, which I thought might turn out to be a positive for me, so I didn't mention it. I waited as she glared at me. Drest watched the two of us without saying anything.

"What's your name?" she asked, leveling her eyes suspiciously at me.

"Bryn," I replied, keeping my eyes locked on hers; I had nothing to hide.

"I'm Decima," she replied and then turned to look at Drest. "Are you both ready to go?"

We replied in the affirmative.

"Good," she said, reaching into the black bag that was slung over her shoulder and across her chest. "We just have to do something else first."

"What's that?" Drest asked.

From her bag, Decima revealed a t-shaped wand with two metallic balls on the ends. She also produced two pairs of sunglasses from of the bag. She looked to me first.

"These will change your eye color permanently. It's absolutely random, so as not to take your personal preference into account. We don't want anyone to be able to recognize you."

"Alright," I replied. I liked the sound of anonymity.

"I'm going to flash this in your eyes. You'll need to wear sunglasses for a while, as your eyes will be sensitive to sunlight. By this evening, the change will have occurred and you'll no longer be light-sensitive."

I nodded.

"Are you ready?" she asked.

"I guess so," I replied, holding my breath.

"It won't hurt," she promised, and before I knew what had happened, I was suddenly blind. I blinked against the darkness that lingered only for a fraction of a minute. I felt her press a pair of glasses in my hand.

"Put those on," she commanded, and I quickly did so. The light in the room alone was already searing.

I watched through the black lenses as she did the same thing to Drest and then looked at the wrist band she wore.

"Time to go," she said.

Drest and I followed silently, our hands empty and our sunglasses covering our eyes. I pressed my hand to my pocket. I could feel that the small compass Quillan had given me was securely in its place.

Decima stepped out of the doorway and crouched down against the outside wall, white like all of the others in the old world. I followed her with Drest right behind me. I looked up and behind us and saw that somehow, we were on the outside of the sterile white subdivision I'd run my way through the night before. I was suddenly thankful for the sunglasses' barrier between the bright white and my sensitive eyes. Even with the glasses, the sun bouncing off the shiny surface of the wall made them water.

"We have to cover a lot of ground today," Decima whispered.

I nodded. It didn't matter how sore I was, how many blisters I may have had on my feet, it was time to go. Besides, energy wasn't something I was lacking that morning.

"How far?" Drest asked.

She shrugged. "Fifteen, twenty miles to the first checkpoint? We'll need to make it by nightfall."

"Let's go," I replied.

Decima smiled, her mouth pulling into a sidewise grin as she clapped me on the shoulder and started running from tree to tree in the dim forest that butted up to the subdivision. She took, prancing over fallen limbs and around trees like a gazelle.

I followed her steps, careful not to trip on the roots that reached up out of the ground between the tall trees. I could hear Drest quietly on my heels, but we didn't say anything to one another as we swiftly put the glossy world behind us and pushed further into the forest.

Under the canopy of green, the light had filtered so much that I wondered if the sunglasses were a necessity, but I wasn't brave enough to risk taking them off. I kept my eyes focused on the ground beneath my feet, watching each step I took so I wouldn't fall. This was a completely unadulterated place; not even the Rangers ventured into them to deforest them in any way. Nature was left to do what it wanted here, and the result was a dappled green paradise. Birds flew away from us and little rodent-like creatures that I had never seen before scurried from our path.

We hiked up steep paths that seemed to reach up to the sky, but we never caught a glimpse of the inevitable blue beyond the green overhead. The exertion was too extreme to allow for conversation, but although I gasped for breath as the climb took us higher and higher into the mountains, I knew that they were free breaths, and the burning in my lungs meant that I was just that much closer to independence.

The ground was soft beneath our feet and as we climbed, the wind became cooler, and the air thinner. I shivered against the chill, thankful for the embrace of the trees, their green leaves cascading from the branches as the lacy fronds of the ferns at our feet brushed against us like the softest velvet.

Decima finally stopped at the summit of the hill we had been mounting and she turned to look down at both of us. She smiled knowingly as she waited. I climbed the last few steps before coming to a stop beside her; I could hear Drest right behind me.

"Oh!" I gasped as my eyes took in the view. I looked quickly behind me, and found that what had seemed like a steep hill must really have been a mountain, because in front of me was a sight I had never seen before.

Looking from the lofty zenith, we could see rolling hills that even in the bright sunlight seemed to look blue. Foggy mists wound between the soft peaks and a reverential calm naturally settled over us.

"Pretty great, huh?" Decima asked.

We nodded; we were speechless.

"This is my favorite part of the trek," she explained. "Nobody ever expects it, and it never fails to surprise even me—and I've seen it dozens of times."

"It looks like it goes on forever, doesn't it?" Drest asked, whistling through his teeth.

"Yeah," I agreed in an awed whisper.

"Unfortunately it doesn't, but it does go on for a long time," Decima said. "Follow me. I've got some food and supplies stashed on the other side. We'll eat and then keep moving."

I started after her as she began to trek down the other side of the slope. We climbed down about ten feet or so and then she suddenly disappeared. I stopped and looked around.

"Uh, Decima?" I called out.

She poked her head around the corner of a cave and smiled. "Come on," she replied before disappearing again.

I giggled under my breath and followed her lead. I didn't have to turn around to know that Drest was right behind me. I could hear him chuckling at her too. We slid down the side of the rock and soon came to rest at the mouth of the cavern.

"Here," Decima said, tossing a coat at me.

I caught it and flipped it around to slide my arms into it. She tossed another to Drest.

"Food," she said, tossing something else at us.

My hands instinctively grasped the object and I read the label on the otherwise nondescript package: *Fried Rice and Eggroll*. It was one of those packet meals kept for emergency reasons. I looked at Drest who slid down to the cave floor and had begun opening his. Decima was eating hers in silence.

I sank down onto my heels, tearing the top of the package off. Inside there was a small package that read *Activation Tab*. I peeled it open and dropped the pink colored tablet into the larger package and felt the contents heat up under my hands. I let my mind wander, and my eyes wandered with it. I could take my glasses off here, shaded from the sun as we were.

The landscape that trellised down the mountainside was green in a way that I had never seen before. Our finely manicured cities of white and chrome included trees and shrubs, but they were nothing compared to what my eyes fell on now. The mountains looked like they were covered with soft, green cotton. The blue sky dipped down and caressed its smoky gray clouds along the ridges of trees. Rolling crests copied each other over and over; they seemed to go on forever.

"Welcome to the Appalachians," Decima said, with a nod towards the cave opening and a knowing smile on her face.

"The Appalachians?" Drest asked.

I turned the unfamiliar word over in my head.

She nodded. "That's what they're called."

"App-a-lach-ians," I sounded out carefully, feeling the strange pronunciation roll around my tongue.

"You're from what used to be called North Carolina," she said.

Drest and I looked at each other, and I guessed that my look of confusion mirrored his. I'd never heard of this place: North Carolina.

Decima chuckled good-naturedly under her breath. "You'll get the hang of it all soon," she promised. "There are libraries and schools in the Republic—a wealth of knowledge and you'll learn things you never thought possible."

I raised an eyebrow at her.

She winked at me. "I promise."

Chapter 8

Six Months Later, or The End of the Journey: Ariston

A very informal semi-circle formed around Ariston as he pulled a book from the tattered bag resting at his feet. He moved his fingers between the yellowed and battered pages, thinned with age. He had copied the contents word-for-word in another, sturdier book, but something about this volume was special; its antiquity seemed to resonate with his students, or at least he'd hoped.

It was hot; the kind of Texas heat that seeps through cloth, the kind of heat that clings to skin. Ariston wiped the back of his hand across his forehead and looked up from the book. For the most part, the students were waiting for him to start. As usual, the girls were more attentive than the boys as they sat in front of their attractive teacher. He sighed almost inaudibly.

"Alright," he began. "What did we talk about last time?"

"The Declaration?" an overly-eager girl responded. She was probably fifteen.

"Yes," Ariston replied patiently. "What about it?"

"Well, that America had to tell England that they wanted to be free?"

He nodded. "That's right. Today we're going to start committing the document to memory."

He ignored the few groans from his "class" as they sat around on the worn floor of the mobile home that served as the schoolhouse.

"I know, I know," he sympathized. "But books may not always be around. We have to remember these things. Okay? Repeat after me: 'When, in the course of human events...'"

The class recited the line back to him.

He continued on, pausing to allow the small group of teens to repeat his words from time to time. "'...it becomes necessary for one people to dissolve the political bands which have connected them with another...'"

68

For half an hour, Ariston led the group in their memorization of the first part of the *Declaration of Independence*, before he was suddenly interrupted.

"Ugh! Why do we have to do this?" one of the boys groaned.

Ariston exhaled in a slow, steady breath. He carefully closed the book in his lap without looking at the teen. He pinched the top of his nose and counted to ten in his head, attempting to stifle the anger that dismissive teens never failed to stir in him.

"Because, *Tarquin*, this is the type of material *they* are banning," he said, waving the book in the air at the boy. The rest of the class fell completely silent, watching one and then the other with awkward glances. "If we don't remember these words, they could be lost forever. What happens when *they* decide to come into the Republic and take it over?"

"Ah, Texas is fine. They can't come in here and take it over," Tarquin replied with a shrug.

Ariston stood from the ratty orange folding chair and walked over to the wall behind him on which hung a faded map of what used to be called the United States. He had long ago marked new boundaries and notated the fallen states, now under the umbrella of the great Society to the north.

He jabbed a deadly finger at what once had been a free state. "That's what Tennessee thought." He glared at his students. Some watched wide-eyed, while others looked away. "That's what Kentucky thought. And Ohio. Michigan. Illinois."

Tarquin shifted nervously where he sat.

Ariston sighed heavily and shook his head in disgust. "Class, you're dismissed." He couldn't deal with them today.

The handful of teens hurriedly stood up, gathered their belongings and filed out of the miniscule temporary building. As they stepped into the sun, it was apparent that their clothes were different shades of brown and grey, but all relatively worn. That was life on a border town. Most of these students wouldn't be around for more than a handful of weeks; their parents often headed southward into the more prosperous center of the Republic of Texas. These were the new ones, like Tarquin, who believed that Texas was a magical place and completely immune to the outside world. It was useless sometimes, to try and convince them otherwise.

"Get mad at them again?" a sultry voice asked out of nowhere.

Ariston turned to see Kallisto standing nearby, a round basket at her hip, on her way to the Laundromat no doubt. Her dirty blonde hair stood out against the grey tank top which had once been black, and the khaki pants she wore almost looked like they had been painted on her shapely legs. She wore a belt with a holstered pistol around her waist. She was smirking at him.

He sighed again. "Yeah," he replied, running a hand through his hair before settling it on his hip in frustration.

She laughed under her breath. "They're kids," she offered by way of an explanation and stared at him for long unsettling minute.

"I know," he replied; he wasn't much older than they were at twenty-five. He refused to believe their age was an excuse.

"Don't sweat it."

"In this heat?" he joked tiredly, looking up at the sky through squinted eyes. It was a perfect blue, which was beautiful, but also meant that there were no clouds promising rain or shade anytime in the near future.

"Right," she laughed, tugging her basket further up on her hip and sauntering off to the Laundromat at the center of town.

He watched her without longing, as she walked away from him. She was attractive, he couldn't deny that, but there was something that didn't sit well with him. It always seemed as if she were a cat ready to pounce on a mouse. She was watchful and liked to sit back and see how a situation unfolded. He was fairly sure that she got exactly what she wanted. Every time.

He looked away and slowly turned back to the small building that served as the school. The Education Department had asked for volunteers to serve half-year terms on the border, a relatively sparse place. It didn't keep families from living there off and on; aiding new refuges into the Republic—there were always people like him and Kallisto, Texans willing to move north to the barren border. Some of these people had children who had to be taken care of while their parents were educated during the day, and many refugees were minors. The school was a glorified daycare; Ariston had been there for six months.

He stood in the little temporary building with the sparse and worn furnishings. He ran his fingers along the edge of the letter he had received earlier that day:

Your service has been greatly appreciated. The Education
Department would like to thank you for volunteering in this
position. Your replacement will follow this letter in a month, at
which time you shall be relieved from your current position and
recalled to the capitol.

He glanced up through the dingy window and watched as the
bright green mesquite trees swayed in the summer wind. It may
have been hot and relatively dirty, but at least there was some
green to the landscape. In the northern part of Texas, the grass was
green and the mesquite trees grew close to the ground. It wasn't
naturally a dusty, barren place, but without cultivation, the rugged
paths that the small community had cut into the landscape
consistently sent dust into the air. When mixed with sweat in the
un-air conditioned heat, it turned to a stubborn mud. He would be
happy to return to a more interior location, where the students were
more permanent, where he could affect more change and imbue the
impressionable minds with the promise that the Republic
represented.

He caught a glimpse of himself in the fragment of mirror that hung
on the wall over the sink to his right. His auburn hair was
haphazardly lying over his forehead, and his bright jade colored
eyes – so many people found unnerving in their odd color and
intensity – were still intense with frustration.

With the heel of his palm he scrubbed ineffectively at a smudge of dirt that had made it onto his cheek at some point. He didn't consider himself attractive, but he could tell that the women and girls—and some boys—around him disagreed. It was obvious, when they flipped their hair, arched their backs, and giggled like hyenas, that they were attracted to him. He preferred to ignore them, although it didn't always work to deter them.

A sharp rapping on the door shook him from staring at his reflection in the broken glass.

"Got another group comin' in. Look alive, man!" Bion yelled through the closed door.

"I'm coming," Ariston replied, grabbing his bag and slinging it across his chest, sliding his hatchet inside the pocket before he joined his friend outside.

"Hey." Bion held his hand up for a high five. Ariston slapped it and turned towards the compound's front gate.

"Who else is going out?" Ariston asked.

"Me," a familiar voice called.

He and Bion turned around and found Kallisto walking up, a large knife now stuck into the top of her boot. Bion grinned at her, but Ariston turned away as she joined them. He started walking towards the gate with the other two following behind.

"How long has this group been out?" She asked.

"Six months or so?" Bion replied, checking the magazine of his pistol.

"That's pretty quick. How many?" Ariston asked.

"Two," said Bion.

Ariston stopped in his tracks and looked back at his friend. Kallisto watched both men carefully.

"Just two?" He asked.

Bion shrugged. "It's getting harder to get people out."

"Or harder to convince them to leave," Kallisto mumbled under her breath with a sideways glace to Ariston.

He shook his head. "It's just because they don't know."

She nodded but said nothing more.

Ariston turned and headed for the gate which was guarded by two sentries. "We're going to the lookout for a new group," he said.

The guards nodded and opened the gates for the trio. There were pickets in the trees, watching the fields and hills around the borderlands, ready to send up the signal at the first sign of trouble. Ariston, Kallisto, and Bion headed for the highest point in the region, affectionately called "The Lookout" for obvious reasons. They didn't speak, or rather Ariston and Kallisto didn't speak; Bion always seemed to have something to say.

Ariston ignored his chatter as they climbed the summit and looked down to the river valley that snaked its brown way through the green-brown brush. The banks of the river were red against the water where it had receded in the sun. Rocks that would be invisible during the winter were peeking out of the water and served as stepping stones for the small group of four coming their way: two new refugees and two guides. They did not see their watchers.

Chapter 9

Bryn

We followed the winding river, Decima leading the way. Another man had met up with us that morning, but he did not tell me his name, nor did he introduce himself to Drest. He seemed to be content with his anonymity. He was just the last in a long series of strangers we'd met along the way; at this point, we were used to meeting new, strange people.

"We're almost there," Decima said and looked up at a cliff overhanging the river valley.

We had been out for more than six months, and it felt like an eternity. I envied Drest; he was so patient that he didn't seem to mind the monotonous pace of our travels. I wondered if that kind of patience came with age.

"What's that?" Drest asked suddenly, nodding toward the top of the tallest cliff.

Decima squinted against the hot sun even though she wore sunglasses to protect them. *"That* is our envoy. They're going to escort us into the territory."

My eyes caught the movement of three people: a willowy blonde woman, a giant redheaded man, and another man who stood still while his companions moved about. He was smaller than the other man but looked about as solid as the rock face he stood upon. The three did not make a move to help us as we clamored up the cliff.

Decima pulled herself up to the top of the cliff and finally one of the three reached down to help drag her up. It was the redheaded guy, who wore a giant smile.

"Thanks, Bion," Decima said.

He chuckled and shrugged, "Least I can do," he replied. He and Decima helped our other guide, and then Drest, up to the zenith.

They dragged me up last of all, Bion commenting about how light I was. I smirked. His eyes lingered on my face for a moment, as if he recognized me but couldn't figure out why.

The blonde woman looked both me and Drest up and down. "An old man and a girl," she said, raising an eyebrow at Decima. "I guess there were slim pickings."

Decima and Bion howled with laughter. "I can't bring hot guys back every time, Kallisto," Decima said. "Everyone needs their freedom, not just the ones you'd like to drag off to bed."

Kallisto gave her a one shoulder shrug.

"Are we ready?" the stockier man asked suddenly. He was clearly finished with the playful banter between the women.

His stared at me, and I could see my reflection mirrored in the lenses that he wore. He wasn't very tall, probably about average height for a man, but I was still shorter, and my newly jet black hair stood in spikes all over my head. He couldn't see the reflection of my new eyes behind my glasses, of course, but had he seen them, I guessed he would have reacted like everyone else had–with mild shock at best.

When Decima had changed our eyes before we left the bunker, Drest's became a brown so dark that it was hard to distinguish the irises from the black pupils within. Mine, on the other hand, had changed to an icy blue, so light that they looked unnatural. My pupils stood out like blemishes against them. Decima told me that they freaked her out, and I watched as Drest initially shifted uncomfortably under my gaze.

"We're good to go," Decima replied.

Chapter 10

Six months. It had taken us six months to make it to the border. I was happy, relieved, and excited for what lay in my future.

"Hey kiddo," Drest said to me as I walked out of the bathroom, rubbing my head with a towel.

We were bunking in a long, thin building that sat on concrete blocks. There were no floor springs in this building like we had always had up north, but after walking on the solid earth for so long, floor springs would have been a strange and unwelcome sensation below our feet anyway.

They offered to give us separate quarters—there were two such buildings outfitted for this purpose, ready to hold up to twenty people at a time—but that seemed like a waste. Drest and I were so used to sleeping near one another by now that it would have been unsettling to be alone.

"Your turn," I said. "You won't believe how great it feels."

He grinned. "They dropped off some food while you were in there. Said to rest up and take our time. We'll camp here for a few weeks. Apparently some of the settlers here are moving inward then and we'll just go with them."

I nodded. "Sounds good."

He left me with one of the two trays of food and I soon heard the shower water flowing. Drest moved with greater ease now, as if all the time on his feet had worked any stiffness out of his aging body. He was brighter, happier, and seemed healthier.

I felt better too. I felt stronger—emotionally and physically—as if I could conquer anything. I could think about Quillan's death without hurting now, or rather, I only thought about him, not that horrible day. He was a pleasant, warm memory most of the time. There were moments when something would trigger a reminder and I would think of him, but it had been six months so the regret and remorse had faded. I comforted myself with the knowledge that he'd want it that way. I could also lift a lot more and I'd had my share of challenges along the way. I hadn't expected how the journey would harden me.

Chapter 11

Two Weeks into the Journey

We had only been walking for a couple of weeks, stopping at camps along the way where food, new friends, and little luxuries like showers were waiting for us. Everything had seemed the same for a while. The Appalachians were beautiful, but after my initial discovery of their blue slopes and green forests, I longed for another powerful experience with nature. I got it when we came to the Potomac. Sparkling blue and flanked with the same kind of green that covered the mountains, the river ran smooth where we met it, but as we traveled along its banks, it churned with intensity unlike anything I'd ever seen in my life.

I was captivated by its majesty when Drest suddenly gasped.

"What is it?" I asked immediately. His foot appeared to be stuck.

"I'm caught on something," he said and looked at Decima. She stepped forward until I held my hand up to her.

"I've got it," I said, pulling a red tool out of my pocket. It had several different instruments concealed inside. Decima had laughed at me when I called it a *Switch* Army knife.

I dropped to a knee and cut the vine away from his ankle. "Are you okay?" I asked.

He nodded stoically. I knew he had a bad ankle, but he never complained about it. I frequently caught him rubbing it when we settled down some nights. Drest wasn't the complaining type.

"Are we good to keep going?" Decima asked.

"Yes," he replied. "I'll be fine."

"There's a settlement just over there," she said, pointing towards an old bridge that had once arched over the river but now rested in incomplete peace.

I squinted and looked out over the shambles of a town that had once stood on the river bank. A thin line of smoke rose like a ribbon from its edge. I hoped it was a campfire.

The settlement was mostly temporary like most of the ones we'd stopped at along the way. Some people had taken up residence in burnt-out buildings while others had set up a few tents. The latter group had been passing through, like us, but had decided to stay a while. The river provided water and food, nearby fruit trees grew wild, and someone had planted a vegetable garden.

We were immediately greeted by the people who lived there—Decima had contacts everywhere. To my relief, the fire was in fact a campfire, over which several fresh fish were hung to smoke. I shook hands with a couple of people, including a girl of about thirteen, before wandering off to the riverbank where tall reeds grew out of the soggy soil.

It was quiet there and the water lapped lazily at the muddy bank. At our first checkpoint, I'd been given a backpack full of tools and supplies. For the first time, I pulled the machete out of the pack and drew it from its sheath. A glint of light from the setting sun shone across its blade as I struck the first reed. The knife was sharp and cut through the fibrous green plant as if it were little more than paper. I tossed the reed onto the ground.

"Gah!" a voice exclaimed.

I turned abruptly at the sound and saw the girl I'd said hello to when we'd arrived. "Sorry," I replied. "Watch out there." I tossed another reed onto the pile and turned back to the plant.

"What are you doing?" she asked, pushing her long straight hair over her shoulder.

I glanced at her as I tossed another reed onto the pile. "I don't know," I replied honestly.

"Mind if I watch?"

I shrugged. "Don't mind at all. What's your name?"

"Guinevere," she replied before quickly adding, "but I hate it. It's so girly."

"How about this?" I asked, grunting as I threw another reed onto the pile, "What do you *want* me to call you?"

"Gwen is fine," she answered, taking a seat on a nearby rock.

I looked over my shoulder and grinned at her. "Gwen it is then."

She smiled.

I cut a final reed and used it as a walking stick though the mud. Rummaging through my pack, I found a ball of extra thick cord and some matches.

"I think I could survive out of this thing for weeks," I mumbled to myself, but Gwen heard me and giggled. I smiled at her. "So what's your story?"

She shrugged as I cut lengths of cord.

"Come on, everyone's got a story," I prompted, striking a match and burning the ends of the cord so they wouldn't fray.

"I was born out here," she replied. "I live with my aunts, and I really want to go to Texas."

I chuckled under my breath. "Don't we all?"

I split two of the reeds down the center and laid them over the curved edge of the central reed. I handed it to Gwen with a, "Here, hold this please."

She did so and sighed. "Do you...? Do you think I could go with you?"

I wrapped a length of the cord over the far end of the bundle before taking it back from her. "No," I answered, "that wouldn't be a good idea." I sat down and wound more cord around the middle of the bundle.

"Why does everyone say that?" she whined.

I chuckled. "Probably because it's true." I smiled at her and patted her hand. "It's hard growing up sometimes."

She sighed again. I lifted the bundle up with one hand and examined it for any curves.

"Seriously though," Gwen said. "*What* are you making?"

"A wooden sword," I replied matter-of-factly, "or something similar."

"How do you know how to do that?"

"I *do not* know."

Chapter 12

Present Day

It was months later and the reed sword was long gone. Drest was in the shower room and I sat on one of the bunks we had been provided with. I devoured the food on the tray, even dragging the piece of toast against its surface to soak up all of the gravy from the potatoes.

I thumbed through the small leather-bound book of poetry I'd received on my journey. I of course knew what poetry was when I received it, but I had never read any like this before. I couldn't get enough. It was dark and sinister, about women named Elizabeth and Annabel Lee. There was one about a black bird that kept knocking on a man's door that I couldn't quite get the point of, but neither could I get it out of my head. The book was precious to me. I smiled at the thought: It was mine, and mine alone; it didn't belong to a group of people and I didn't have to share it with anyone. Once into the interior of the Republic, we were supposed to have many of the same conveniences I had been raised around so my little trove of collected objects—the book, a flint stone, and a woven bracelet—was more novelty than anything, but it was mine and mine alone.

There was a sudden knock at the door. My reaction didn't make any sense, but I looked around as if someone else were in the room before getting up off of the bed and walking to it. I flipped the latch and it swung open easily, despite its rusted hinges. The man I'd seen on the way up to the settlement—I had learned his name was Ariston—stood just beyond the doorway.

"Hi," he said, staring at me strangely.

"Um, hi," I replied, confused. "Is something wrong?"

"No," he replied simply and seemed distracted. "I came to see if you and Drest would like a tour of the camp."

"Oh," I replied, looking over my shoulder. "Well, he's in the shower right now."

Ariston's eyes flashed up to my still wet hair and back down to my eyes. He looked away from me for a split-second before making contact again. I still wasn't used to how unnatural my eyes looked to everyone.

"But," I quickly added, "I'll come along. Hang on just a second."

I turned and let the door slam closed. I skipped over to my bed and pulled my boots onto my feet. I scooped up my little collection of objects and stuffed them into my pack. I slid my book into one of the pockets in my pants.

"Drest!" I called through the closed door, "Ariston's taking me on a tour of the camp. See you in a bit!"

"Okay, kiddo," he yelled back.

I pushed the door open and Ariston turned abruptly at the sound. He reacted to people differently than most. He didn't seem comfortable, and I'd be lying if I said it didn't make me feel a little awkward in his presence. The tendency to want to walk on eggshells around him was significant. I got the sense that he might be one of those men who tended toward the sensitive side of the emotional scale.

"Ready," I said, without waiting for him to say anything.

Nothing had been like I'd expected; in school they'd always scared us away from the borderlands and the wide open. I found it freeing. One night Decima taught us how to catch fish. On another, we stopped by a small tent city of about eight settlers. The accommodations were nothing more than basic tents with dirt floors, but it was always nice to be around a group of people.

Cady—she'd been named after an activist who had fought centuries ago for the equal rights of women—and her wife Martha had given me the little book of poetry that now rested in my pocket. They smiled at each other conspiratorially over the campfire before Cady presented it to me. She'd tied it with some straw, and I loved it at first sight. I rarely felt like a child, but Martha and Cady's manner with me made me remember what I'd been like as a small girl: eager, excited. Somehow I'd lost that along the way to adulthood.

I brushed my fingers against the small tome bulging out of the pocket on the side of my leg and smiled. Martha told me they would be heading back into the interior of the Republic soon. I hoped I'd see them again.

Ariston kept glancing down at me awkwardly as we walked towards the larger buildings of the complex.

"What?" I asked.

"Um," he began, shaking his head slowly, "your...um, your eyes. They're a little unsettling is all."

I snickered, "Yes, I know. I guess it's not really a common color, huh?"

"Not at all," he agreed.

"Leave it to me to get the freaky eyeballs," I joked playfully.

"They're quite beautiful," he said matter-of-factly.

I frowned at the ground. "Thanks."

He shrugged.

The sun beat down on us as we stepped out of the building— Decima had warned us that the heat was just something we'd have to get used to in Texas, apparently the seasons didn't vary much here. Luckily, I still had the glasses that she had given me, so I slipped them on.

"Better?" I joked, looking up at Ariston.

He smiled, and it didn't look like he did that often. He had a kind of awkward way of turning his lips up, as if the movement were uncomfortable for him. Still, maybe that was the important part: that he was trying.

Everything was so brown—I'd noticed that when we were coming into the camp. Sitting on the top of a bluff that overlooked a river below, the small settlement possessed all of the essentials to life. The people lived communally: There was a central laundry building, a cafeteria, and a recreation center.

"The settlement is funded by taxes from the Republic," Ariston told me. "The transition between the world you come from and freedom has been deemed very important to all Texans."

I snickered under my breath.

"What is it?" he asked.

"You're very formal, is all. I don't mean to laugh at you; it's just that I haven't heard someone speak that way in a while."

"Oh," he replied, looking surprised. "I really only do it for newcomers. Most adults have a hard time transitioning—conversationally."

I picked a rock up and rolled it around between my thumb and forefinger. I tossed it towards a little creek and chuckled ironically.

"What are you laughing about now?" he asked.

I shook my head. "Those reeds over there? I made a sword out of those a few months ago. It reminded me of a girl I met on the Potomac. Her name was Gwen."

"Tell me about her," he commanded gently.

"She tried to follow us out of her settlement. She found me cutting reeds and hung around while I worked with them. We talked for a while and the next thing I knew, she wouldn't leave my side. She followed me around like a little puppy and tried to sneak away to follow us. Of course she had to stay behind." I smiled, thinking of her. "She was a cute kid."

"What did you mean by a sword? Where is it now?"

I shrugged and narrowed my eyes as I looked at the horizon.

"Just a sword," I replied. "I lost it somewhere along the journey."

"Hmm," he said before looking off into space.

I remembered exactly what had happened to the sword. I had had it up until about two weeks ago. A group of men threatened us. The first came at Drest, who held his own well enough. Decima shot her own assailant in the side of the head when he managed to kick her feet out from underneath her.

I held the sword in my hand, knowing that I wouldn't be able to break bones with the weapon, just looking for a way to protect myself. In an arching sweep I struck him under the chin, but it seemed like it only angered him more. He charged at me and I hit him again in the back of the head, but he was a fighter. He caught my sword as I pulled it away. He was bigger than the other two, so he was able to easily break it under his foot.

The reeds splintered as he laughed. He came at me and instead of dodging that time, I ran up his bent knee and vaulted over his shoulders. My hand landed on one of the sword's halves. I grasped it without thinking. He turned and started running toward me and I drove my half into his chest. The look in his eyes was one of shock that I'd never forget. It was rivaled only by Decima's look of surprise, although my excuse as a guard trainee—not a complete lie—seemed enough to satisfy her.

It was certainly not the first time I'd killed someone. When I had driven the sword fragment into the man, I didn't cringe away from the feeling. I didn't look to Drest for support. I dusted my hands off and walked away.

The sound of approaching footsteps distracted me from my memory.

"Hey there," the gorgeous blonde greeted. Her name was Kallisto, and it was pretty clear what her intentions for Ariston were.

I looked up at her, nodded a greeting, and smiled.

"Hi," he replied, a little more relaxed with her than with me.

"What are you two up to?" she asked, looking dismissively at me. Like Ariston, she had to look down to look into my eyes. I wondered if she also didn't look down at me in that more metaphorical sense; she was hard to read.

"I'm just giving Bryn the tour of the place," he explained.

"Oh," she replied, and I couldn't tell if she was happy about it or not.

I wanted to tell her that I had no interest in Ariston; that I wouldn't be a challenge and I wouldn't stand in her way if she wanted to pursue him, but I thought that maybe he wouldn't appreciate it. He didn't seem to have any more interest in her than I had in him, that is to say that I knew we'd get along well and he was a really nice guy, but I wasn't in a place where romance made sense.

I also understood that such a statement would likely bruise his ego. I didn't want to hurt anyone.

"Are you headed to the chow hall soon?" He asked.

Kallisto jerked her hair into a ponytail and nodded. "Yeah," she replied.

"Cool," he responded and gestured toward to me to keep walking. I stepped away from Kallisto with a nod to her and he fell in right beside me. "I'll catch up with you later," he said.

"I'll send you a dirty text," she called.

He shook his head but waved, adding, "See you!"

I smiled over my shoulder at him as he caught up. "No interest there?" I asked.

He smiled and shook his head. "She's a good friend," he replied.

"She knows what she wants," I replied as we came to the end of the one road that ran through the settlement. We stood on the edge of the bluff, looking towards the interior of the Republic of Texas.

The land seemed to stretch out forever in rugged brown-green tones, spiked with the bright, almost yellow-green of a native tree with their twisted limbs and trunks, spread wide and far as if to absorb all of the sun—and all of the sparse rainfall—that the climate would have to offer. Ariston caught me looking at them.

"Those are Mesquite trees," he said. "They're extremely hardy. They're one of the only trees that can live in drought conditions. They draw water up from deep in the ground."

"I guess everything that lives out here has to be a survivor," I mused.

He nodded, and looked at me meaningfully. "You have to be a survivor to get here in the first place."

I smiled and looked away. He was right. "So why are you here? I mean, I'm glad there are people like you who want to help—well, people like me—but what do you do here?"

"Those are two different questions you know," he replied, smirking at me.

I shrugged. I didn't feel like playing games, even harmless little flirtations of a game. My life had been full of such things. I was ready to be real and for the realism of the world around me.

"I'm here because I believe in the cause. I believe people have a right to be free: to make their own choices, to decide who they love, where they work, how they experience their own soul. As for what I do here, I'm a teacher. The Education Department sends two teachers here to help usher people into their new lives. I teach the kids, and Ena, whom you haven't met yet, teaches the adults."

"I admire your passion," I admitted.

He smiled.

"What about the other people who live here?" I asked, turning around and looking at the small settlement.

Most of the buildings were temporary structures, either hauled here decades ago or left behind by another group of people, where the buildings became an afterthought of a town. It was sparser than any of the places we'd stopped at along the way, as if just being there was a hazard to your health.

Most of the buildings were metal resting on blocks of some sort— cement and wood—that allowed them to seemingly hover above the ground. They had been various shades of color once: light blue, white, grey, brown, yellow, but now they were so sun-bleached and rusted that they all resembled one another. I frowned looking at them. Freedom came with a price, I knew that, but I didn't realize that freedom would be so beaten up, so dirty.

"They all have their reasons," he replied, turning to face the buildings as well. "Some of them like the adventure; others are here on a contract with their employers. Kallisto, for instance, is one of the technical people around here. She makes sure our phones and our computers are always working."

He pulled an old looking phone out of his pocket. I had only seen pictures of the touchscreen devices; they seemed so antiquated compared to what I had left behind.

"They still make those?" I asked automatically.

He smiled. "Not where *you're* from. We run off older technology here—there's no need for the high-tech gear you're used to if nobody's listening in all the time."

I frowned, because it was the truth. I hadn't been away from that life for long, but in that short time, I'd come to value my privacy in a more fierce manner than I ever expected I would. Six months ago, The Government listening in on a phone conversation was par for the course. Now it seemed like the ultimate violation of something absolutely elemental to my being as a person.

I'd never thought that way before.

"What is it?" he asked quietly.

I shook my head. "Things are changing quickly." I glanced up at him and his eyes made me think of Quillan for a flash of a moment.

I sighed at the similarity that he shared with my friend. Ariston misinterpreted the sigh.

"It's hard on everyone at first—except for the little ones. They think it's an adventure," he said softly.

I envied the little ones—I hoped they would have a life free from the pain that I'd experienced. I smiled. "I bet they do."

He looked down at me then and cocked his head to the side. "Come with me. I want to show you something."

I narrowed my eyes at him. "Hmm...I'm not sure," I replied with a smile, but of course I'd go with him.

He grasped my hand and pulled me along to a building that was almost reflective it was so white, and I let him. He took the steps in two strides. I had to climb each one; I'm short. Looking back over his shoulder at me excitedly, he grinned as he pulled the door open with a jerk.

The cool air of the interior hit me in the face. It had a damp, dark quality to it, as if we were in a cave. It felt good. Everything looked like it had seen better days; the carpets were threadbare and the furniture seemed to have collected dust for decades. The walls were covered with large maps, posters, and scraps of artwork and handwritten slivers of paper.

"Where are we?" I asked.

"This is the school, or what qualifies as such," he replied, looking around. "I'll miss this place, believe it or not."

"When do you leave?" I asked.

"In a couple of weeks when you do," he replied with a quick smile.

"You're getting better at that, you know."

"At what?"

"Smiling."

He was clearly confused. I walked over to the large map on the wall, giving him a chance to process what I'd just said.

"What do you mean?" He asked.

"It seems you're disappointed by people pretty often. You're smiling today more than you usually do. Am I right?"

I didn't turn around to look at him.

"It's that obvious?"

I shrugged.

He dropped the subject and walked to one end of the building. "Come here," he said.

I followed and stood over him as he pulled a metal door up from the floor. Lodged red dust puffed away from the matted carpet's rough-cut edges. Ariston reached up to the counter that ran along one wall of the thin building and grasped a large industrial looking flashlight with a clamp on the end. He looked up at me and smiled.

"Come on," he encouraged and started climbing down a ladder that was hidden in the shadow.

He shone the light on the steps so I could see well enough to get a good footing. I lowered myself into the small square hole and was immediately struck by the change in temperature. It was even cooler under the building.

I climbed down ten or so steps before landing on the soft ground below. I looked at Ariston. "What is this place?"

He swung the light around to a tunnel that stretched out from the space we stood in. "This is an escape route," he explained. "We've never needed it, but it's nice to know it's here. This is also where we keep a lot of our original documents." He swung the light around to the closest wall.

He handed the light to me and its beam danced over the spines of books and stacks of papers there. Ariston reached just beyond the circle of illumination and fiddled with something near the ground. Suddenly, the space was consumed by a bright light from a gas lantern. He smiled at me.

"I thought you might appreciate this," he said.

"And why's that?"

He glanced down at my leg where my book was clearly stashed in one of my pockets. "You like books," he replied simply.

I watched him carefully for a minute—he didn't miss anything. I turned to the shelf and reached for the paper. I pulled my hand back quickly and looked at him for permission.

"You can touch them," he said, clearly seeing me hesitate.

Pulling a book off of the middle shelf, I held it in my hand reverently. I tilted the cover toward the light were the lantern's glow reflected off of the dulled gold paint where the title was pressed into the leather. I'd never seen something so old yet so promising.

"*Anna Karenina*," I read aloud, but in barely more than a whisper.

I gently opened the book, feeling the weight of the front cover fall open into my hand. I ran my fingers over the edges of the sheets of paper and gingerly turned to the first page. I was barely aware of Ariston watching me in the dim light.

"*Happy families are all alike; every unhappy family is unhappy in its own way*," I read and glanced at Ariston. It was a funny way to start a book. I smiled and he smiled back.

"See?" he asked. "I knew you would like it."

Chapter 13

Present Day: Kallisto and Bion

"We can do it," Bion said.

"What do you need?" Kallisto asked.

They sat across from one another at the chow hall. Bion leaned across the table in his intensity, gripping his metal coffee mug like it was trying to escape. A lock of his comically red hair fell across his forehead as he leaned forward. The hair color – which had been changed when he left the old world for the new – was the only thing that softened him enough to keep him from being terrifying. That and the fact that he tended towards the chatty, and whistled just about everywhere he went.

"People," he replied.

Kallisto sat back and crossed her arms, thinking. Her mass of blonde curls had been tugged up into a ponytail at the top of her head, but it didn't show any sign of behaving. She was beautiful; the kind of woman that men lusted after. She was also almost as deadly as he was.

"Well you know I'm in," she replied. "Do you think the rumors are true? Do you think that people are really ready for a revolution?"

"I think so," he replied confidently. "It seems like everyone who escapes now has been to a secret meeting of one sort or another. They're breaking the rules right under the Imperator's nose."

"The fact that they're here makes them rule breakers by nature," she pointed out.

"True," he consented and sat back in his own chair. "Who else?"

She shook her head and shrugged, thinking. "Ariston – obviously – Decima, Edward, Richard, Aeliana, probably Fiedlimid."

He nodded. She had listed off all of the most powerful and the most dedicated voices at the border. If they could just start spreading the idea of freedom northward…

"We can do it," he said. "I just wish I had a little more muscle to throw at it."

"Have a little patience," she replied. "We can make this happen."

Chapter 14

Bryn

We had been in the hole for hours, going over page after page of the documents that lined the hidden underground shelves. There were political documents and works of fiction and poetry, slips of paper that Ariston told me was written music, and the remnants of glossy paper from something called magazines. They were all beautiful.

He pulled a book from the shelf with a tenderness reserved for lovers. Opening the pages of the very thin tome, he began reading it to me.

He spoke with such clarity and his words were like music to my starved ears. *My* ears. I didn't know how long it would take for me to get used to it; personal pronouns still felt wrong from time to time. I tried to concentrate as he spoke, the words and their promise washing over me; filling me with hope.

"We hold these truths to be self-evident, that all men are created equal, that they are endowed by their Creator with certain unalienable Rights, that among these are Life, Liberty and the pursuit of Happiness."

The words were like gold. They lingered in the air, hovering there in their endless potential, even after he'd ceased talking. I was lost in thought when his firm grasp on my hand pulled me from my reverie and we were suddenly running as fast as our feet could carry us through the underground tunnels. I hadn't had the chance to register what was happening before it happened, but I trusted him implicitly, and so we ran.

Away from the ear-splitting, scraping sound of machinery.

I panicked as soon as the sound registered. My heart raced against my ribs. I eagerly gripped his hand back with my own as we ran for dear life.

"Go, go, go!" Kallisto yelled from behind.

The tunnel seemed to have filled with people pushing away from the horrible sound. As we ran, I thought briefly of Drest, wondering where he was in the melee.

"In here!" Ariston shouted over the noise and led us into a larger room further into the ground.

Bion—the redheaded man I met when I first arrived—brought up the rear and closed a heavy metal door behind the last of the group. The scraping of the machinery diminished behind its metal plating. I looked around with dread in my heart.

Ariston had said that they had never needed the tunnels as an escape route. Clearly there had never been a reason for anyone to attack the settlement before.

Bion tinkered with a box near the door. It was some sort of makeshift contraption—metal boxes and wires that ran beneath the steel door. It looked too handcrafted to be much good, but he seemed to know exactly what he was doing. I could only guess it was a rigged explosive system.

"What are those?" I asked Ariston, nodding toward Bion.

He looked down at our clasped hands and dropped mine before answering. "Explosive charges," he replied. "They will collapse the tunnels."

As if to reinforce the point, the ground shook as soon as Bion pushed a couple of buttons. Loose dirt from the ceiling drifted down on our heads for a brief moment before everything settled.

I glanced around at the small group of people. There was a mother cradling her teenage son as if he were a baby. He was injured, but not severely. Bion was talking to a tiny woman, whose animated nodding could only mean that she was agreeing with what he said. There was a small group of kids chattering together while their parents hovered nearby with worried looks on their faces. Kallisto picked up a lantern and walked towards us as a sudden wave of relief rushed over me.

"Drest!" I called and didn't wait for him to respond. I rushed over to him and threw my arms around his neck. He laughed into my hair.

"Are you okay, kiddo?" he asked, pushing me back to get a good look at my face.

"Yes," I replied. "Are you?"

He nodded. "I'm fine. I've got Kallisto to thank for that, though. We set out to look for you and the boy there—" he pointed to

Ariston "—and as soon as we saw them land, she knew exactly where to run to."

"Wait, what?" I asked as my assumptions started to take on a new reality. "What do you mean you saw them land?"

"A battalion of troops and a couple of big metal vehicles—I've never seen anything like them—they had tracked wheels and large forked buckets on one end," he explained, not knowing how to describe tanks from his civilian perspective. "I think there were big guns on the other end. They must be from the Army."

My heart sank. I nodded. "They are."

Chapter 15

"These doors will hold them off," Ariston said, looking around at the group that had gathered in the hole. There were perhaps twenty of us.

I shook my head. "No, they won't," I replied. "Is there another way out of here?"

He stared at me, dumbfounded. "We just collapsed twenty feet of tunnels and we've got a reinforced steel door between us and them. We'll be fine until our reinforcements get here."

"I'm serious," I replied. "We need to keep moving. Is there another way out?"

He glanced over my shoulder at what was probably a doorway, but he wouldn't answer.

The people behind me started talking to each other as I stared at him, Kallisto, and Bion. None of them wanted to believe me, that was evident, but it didn't look like they were ready to suggest that I was lying either.

Kallisto looked at Ariston. "Make the call," she said, tossing a bright yellow phone towards him.

He caught it with one hand and nodded seriously at her, frowning at the gadget in his hand. Whoever was on the other line picked up quickly. Ariston spoke in hushed, hurried tones; his eyes jumped around the room until they locked onto mine. There they froze and I felt other eyes turn to look at me, to see who he stared so intently at.

The attention made me look away. I glanced at Kallisto who had migrated to the opposite side of the room. She was busy making sure our companions were all okay. My eyes moved around the room. Bion chuckled at my behavior like he knew what I was thinking, as if he were oblivious to the danger that dug its way closer towards us as the minutes passed achingly by. I wished he knew what we were up against. He had far too much confidence in his dirt barrier.

Ariston had led us to a large underground bunker, where some canned food and tools were lined up in orderly fashion along several shelves. I looked around for a long stick, or even a garden tool that could be used as a weapon—anything. I was desperate to have something in my hands. It didn't matter how ineffective a makeshift weapon might be in the coming minutes.

Ariston signed off of his communication and turned to the group.

"The Republican Army is sending a company out to rendezvous with us here. A unit will get us into the interior and the rest will hold the borderline here," he began, casting his gaze about the dimly lit room. "They'll be here in a couple of hours."

I sighed.

He continued, "We'll have to stay here until then."

I shook my head and several of the people turned to look at me, including Drest. He walked over to stand next to me.

"What is it, kiddo?" he asked.

I was still shaking my head. "We can't stay here," I replied in a whisper. "Those machines, those tanks—I know what they are—

they're going to get through in the next hour or so. They'll clear a path for the soldiers behind them. Then they'll flood the tunnel and get through the door faster than the Republican company can get here. We have to keep moving."

"You really think so?" he asked.

I nodded in reply and walked over to Ariston. He stood against the rough dirt wall talking to a couple of men I didn't know. He looked down at me with concern.

"We have to keep moving," I said firmly.

He shook his head in protest. "No, the commander said to stay right where we are."

I was already staring at him in defiance. The man next to him shifted from one foot to another, revealing a stack of pipe piled against the wall. I reached around him and grasped one. Holding it up in the light, I looked at it approvingly.

"Ariston," I replied confidently, "you *have* to trust me. We're not safe."

It felt good to have something in my hand—even something as inadequate as a steel pipe. It would work when I had no other weapon within reach. At least I could clock someone in the head with it if it came down to that. I twirled the pipe around in my hand without thinking, as if it were a Down Stick.

Ariston looked at me suspiciously. "Why should I trust you?" he asked.

"Because I know what's out there. The Comitatus Tanks will eat through that soil in an hour. The battalion that's behind them will rush into the tunnel and into this room, and then we'll all be dead. They won't wait around to hear our side of the story," I replied, spinning the stick in my hand again, remembering the feel and the technique—it had been far too long since I'd practiced. "I…I won't go back," I added. "And I'm not ready to die yet."

He watched me through narrowed eyes. The pipe twirled in my hand with an impressive ease. "How do you know how to do that?" he asked.

"That's not the point," I said.

"The hell it's not!" he replied, fire in his eyes.

121

I stood up straighter in response to his raised voice. "Move these people or I will," I said firmly. I looked over my shoulder at where I knew the exit must be.

He glanced from me to the indentation on the wall. "Tell me why first."

"Other than the fact that we're dead if we stand our ground?" I asked, surprised at his reluctance.

"Yes. What makes *your* opinion more valid than the commander's?" He held up the emergency phone in reference.

I looked around at the rest of the people in the room: the motherly looking woman still standing next to Bion, the kids who stopped chattering when Ariston and I started arguing, their parents hovering nearby, Kallisto leaning against one wall, another group of men further away. My eyes caught Drest's. He nodded encouragingly. I sighed and turned back to Ariston.

"I am Bryn Kana Craw Arnaud, Countess, daughter of Regina Diane and Imperator Roland, sister of Melisent, heir apparent to the Government of the States of North America," I answered, feeling the full weight of my full name and title. "I was in training to become the next Regina Guardian."

Bion looked at me with shock in his eyes. Ariston stared warily at me and I didn't dare look around at the rest of the room. Instead, I continued:

"I came seeking peace and a way out of the life I lived. In the months that I've been free of that yoke," I said, borrowing a new word I had just learned left over from the time of an earlier revolution. "In those months, I have learned what it is to live and what it means to honor my own will. I will stand and fight with you if that's what it comes down to, but I'm not too proud to run. And we must run. Those tanks will be here soon, and a battalion of troops after them, but as long as we keep moving we'll be safe."

Ariston looked towards Bion, who turned to look at Kallisto. She nodded at Ariston and walked over to a heavy trunk that sat against the far wall. Tossing the heavy lid open, she pulled a hefty firearm out. She cocked the gun and looked at me. "Let's go," she agreed. "We're trusting you with our lives." She gestured toward the children nearby. "And we're trusting you with our future. Don't disappoint us."

I exhaled in relief. "I won't."

She nodded. "Everyone grab a weapon." Reaching into the trunk, she pulled out a Down Stick. "You'll probably get better use out of this," she said, before tossing it at me.

I dropped the pipe and caught the Stick as my arm came back up. I smiled. "Got some firepower in there for me too?"

The corner of Kallisto's lips pulled up in a sideways smile. "My kind of girl," she replied. She dropped the magazine out of a pistol—something that felt like an antique in my hand—and handed it to me with two other magazines. "Let me show you how to load it."

She slid the magazine into the black pistol and pulled back on the slide. "It's loaded now, just point and shoot." She pointed to a small button on the side. "When you run out, hit this, drop the mag, and slide another one into its place."

I nodded and practiced a couple of times as she watched me. It was certainly a different tool than the ones I was used to dealing with, but I was a quick learner. All around me, the entire room seemed to be buzzing with anxiety.

I was concentrating on the new weapon so much that I didn't notice when Decima stomped towards me. I didn't see her pull her arm back and I didn't see it coming when the back of her hand slapped hard against my cheek, throwing me off balance. I fell on my back just as Kallisto held her arm up to stop Decima from jumping on me.

"You!" she spat, pushing against Kallisto's hold on her. "How dare you!" she yelled.

I stood up, cradling my cheek in my hand. The skin felt hot to the touch, my jaw throbbed, and even my eyeball hurt from the impact.

"Quit it," Kallisto warned.

Drest ran to me and stood between me and the angry Decima.

"How could you go on like that and not tell me?" she demanded. The room had come to a deathly quiet.

I watched her carefully. "Would you have let me come if I had?" I asked quietly.

"No!" was her immediate response. "You've put all of us in danger. You're one of them! Your family is responsible for so much suffering. They want you back and now they've come for you! You, Bryn, have caused this."

Drest stood between us still and slipped his arm behind my back, I think ready grab me if she lunged again. "Does her birth exempt her from wanting freedom?" he asked, his voice filling the room.

"Her birth makes her dangerous company!" Decima countered. "All the time on the road and you couldn't tell me?"

Ariston walked towards us cautiously. "Her birth also makes her an asset," he said. "Think what it means to have a member of the royal family on our side! It's unprecedented." He glanced at me before looking back at Decima. "I understand why she didn't tell you."

Bion sighed and smiled at me. He gave me a little shrug that I didn't understand at the time.

Kallisto looked solemnly from Ariston to Decima and back again. "Which is why they're coming after her so fiercely, I'd bet."

He nodded. "You're probably right." He looked around at us all. "We should get moving then. They surely won't stop."

Chapter 16

At least I'd had a shower. That was my first thought, not that it mattered now. The black earth we trudged through, the dank tunnels, the soggy soil, all of it saturated our clothes, and my hair was soon matted to the sides of my head.

No one asked me about my training as Regina Guardian; they all knew what that meant. There was only one Regina Guardian in an age. Sometimes they were replaced, but it was rare that a Guardian was killed in her line of duty. Society had been built so that the people were about as militaristic as house cats. In contrast, the Regina Guardian—who was constantly at the Regina's side—was the ultimate protector, rivaled by the Imperator Guardian only, her male counterpart.

I was to be Melisent's guardian when she assumed the throne. As her eldest sister, the duty fell to me first. It was a great honor. And my disappearance was an even greater insult to my family and the future of the Society.

We pushed forward and Kallisto led the way. I suspected her job here at the border settlement was more involved than just making sure the computers and the phones still worked. I walked at the back of the group with Drest and Bion—the former wouldn't leave my side and the latter was ready for anything. I admittedly felt better with Bion bringing up the rear. He talked of the American Revolution—the "first revolution" he called it. He talked of the Texan war for independence. He talked of something called the Enlightenment, and Drest appropriately asked questions.

Every few minutes, or whenever he could manage it, Ariston looked over his shoulder at me. The fire in his eyes was clear even in the dimly-lit tunnels that we scurried through like ants. He hadn't been angry for even a moment when he'd found out who I really was. That part shocked me. Instead it was almost as if he burned with more freedom-finding passion than before. I could only guess this had to do with the fact that he now had an ally in a royal family member. The fact that I was the future Regina Guardian was icing on the proverbial cake.

His looks were intense though, and something stirred deep within my soul as it remembered the affect such looks had on me in the past. I was attracted to him physically, but I also found him intriguing: he spoke with an idealism that lacked naivety and I'd never met anyone who was as observant as he was. I found myself wanting to learn more about him.

"Oof!" Drest groaned and reached out towards me automatically as he tipped sideways.

I grabbed Drest's arm to steady him and he smiled sheepishly at me. I smiled back. He'd picked me up in more ways than one—I was a little broken when we'd met—the least I could do was help right him when he took a wrong step. He chuckled at me and himself.

"Are you okay?" I asked.

"Yes," he replied, shaking his head as he leaned against the wall. Bion stopped and waited with us as Drest turned his foot in a circle, moving his ankle around.

"Everything alright?" Ariston asked, nearer to us than I expected him to be.

I glanced up at him and then back to Drest. "We're fine," I replied. "Drest just took a wrong step."

"Are you able to continue?" Ariston asked him.

Drest nodded. "Yeah, I'll be good to go soon."

Ariston looked between the two of us. "We need to get moving," he said before looking down at me. "I don't want to leave anyone behind."

I stared back at him, wishing I'd developed psychic powers somewhere along the way. It would have been nice to know what he was thinking.

"All good?" Kallisto called from the front of the group.

"Yep!" I called back to her trying—in vain—to look over the heads of the people in between us.

She saw what I was doing and smiled at me good-naturedly. "Well come on then!"

I smiled at Drest. "You ready old man?"

He winked at me. "Sure thing, kiddo. Let's get going."

He threw his arm over my shoulders and we started off after the rest of the group, leaving Bion and Ariston to catch up.

Chapter 17

It was nice, traveling the tunnels with a couple of men. They were quiet in a way some women just couldn't be. Ariston gave me a look so intense that it would have melted ice when he passed me and Drest on his way back up to the front of the group with Kallisto. Bion caught up with us but he didn't feel the need for nervous, mindless chatter, and I could be left alone with my thoughts. He did seem to be singing a very old song to himself, but I could handle that. It was nice knowing he was nearby.

Bion and I fell into an easy manner with one another. It was comforting to have him nearby—and I have always been the type to value my personal space. His red hair made him slightly less threatening, but he was an imposing figure nonetheless. His broad shoulders were those of the quintessential soldier, but he always wore a cheerful smile. He reminded me of Quillan, with more authority. I smiled, thinking of my friend…

About eight months ago or so, we had sneaked away once to an underground dance hall—it was literally under the ground—where they played music that time had forgotten. It was soulful and dirty and deep and passionate. He pulled me close in the midst of the rest of the young rebels. If the rebellious crowd that night was any indication as to the impending future, things weren't going to continue on in a way that my family and the rest of the ruling class expected. We were packed in like the salty little fish in the tin can that Decima fed me months later on my trek to Texas.

I smiled remembering it. The air had been thick and the music just made us all want to move to its slow pace and rolling tempo. One of the other boys I danced with there told me it was called the Blues, but I just wanted it to roll over me and through me.

It felt like sex and it felt like freedom.

"Move with the music," the boy had whispered close to my ear, his hands on my hips.

Our bodies moved against each other's and I felt the back of another dancer against mine. We danced in our rebellion and savored every minute of it. It seemed like time ran away from us that night, that hours passed in a single minute within that dark, dusky brown cave. I was anonymous there; not the sister of the future queen, not a killer in training, just me.

"There's more of that when we get out of here," Quillan promised that night as we sneaked away from the dance hall.

There was movement at the front of the long line of evacuees.

"Here we go!" Kallisto called, bringing me back into the present. She held her hand up and the group slowed to a stop in stages. Ariston turned to the rest of us and took a deep breath.

"We're going to head out of the tunnels now," he said. "This should open up on the side of a hill, but I'm not entirely sure. Keep low and keep moving. I've radioed the commander to let him know which direction we'll be heading to."

"Everyone ready?" Kallisto asked.

I nodded along with the rest of them, gripping my Down Stick tightly with one hand and Drest's hand with the other. I felt fueled by my nervous energy. I had no way of knowing how prepared I was for anything outside the tunnel. I had no way of knowing what I was capable of. Drest grinned reassuringly at me. It was always nice to have an optimist along.

"The ankle's all better," he said.

I smiled. "Let's go!"

Chapter 18

"Wow," Bion said, raising his arm to shade his eyes. "That's bright."

"Yes, it is," I agreed as I blinked into the light. The sunlight reminded me of the day my eyes had been changed—it seemed that intense.

"Come on," Ariston said, suddenly appearing at my side.

I took his proffered hand and emerged completely out of the tunnel. I heard a rumbling behind us.

"Oh no," I whispered.

His eyes bore into mine. "The tanks?" he whispered in return.

I nodded.

He whistled low to Kallisto whose head turned swiftly at the sound. He nodded in the southern direction and she nodded back to him.

"Come on then," he replied and pulled me southward.

We were running again. The trees were harder here, their branches whipped against my body. Unlike the foliage I ran through when I escaped my home, these trees didn't give way when they were struck. The wood cut sharp lines across my skin, the branches stinging as they slashed. The ground was harder too. It wasn't covered in moss or soft dirt; it was rocky and the stones threatened to push through the bottoms of my shoes.

I laughed sardonically to myself.

"What?" Ariston asked breathlessly.

I smirked at him as he fought to keep pace with me. "I'd really like to stop running sometime," I replied.

He let out a short burst of laughter. "I bet," he said between breaths. "You will."

I shrugged as I ran under the long-reaching branch. Ahead of me, Kallisto jumped over a felled tree that was simultaneously rotted and bleached under the hot sun, but I expected to see her continue running. Instead she seemed to have disappeared.

"Where's Kallisto?" I asked Ariston.

"I don't know."

A few of the others followed her lead, some easing themselves over the tree while others jumped like she had. None of them reemerged.

"It must drop off there," Bion said from behind us.

"We're about to find out," I replied.

We ran up to the tree and looked over. A large group of people was gathered in the riverbed below—our party and a military detachment.

"The battalion," Ariston said, before jumping over the log and sliding down the embankment.

I followed his lead. Drest and Bion were right behind me. I slid down the sloping dirt, the edge of my boot digging in to the soft soil there.

"Whoa," one of the men said when he caught me.

I looked up, pushed my hair out of my face, and locked eyes with him.

My heart stopped.

It was like life had me on a circular path, and I was on the second revolution of its turning.

Quillan stood before me. He was alive. It was just like before, but nothing like before. He must have been exiled here by the Government, because he looked exactly the same—there was no need for subterfuge when Society knew exactly where they put you. Yet he was different, or maybe I was the one who was different.

He didn't recognize me. My eyes and my hair were so different, I couldn't expect anything less. My skin was tanned and rougher than it ever had been, from my six weeks' unprotected exposure to the sun. I'd lost weight, my face thinner, leaner, more severe when it had been soft and round and the color of porcelain before.

140

"Are you alright?" he asked, looking me over.

I glanced over his shoulder at Ariston who watched me carefully, focused on the change in my behavior.

Should I speak? I thought.

I nodded instead, afraid he'd recognize the sound of my voice. I wasn't ready to have that conversation. He chuckled and glanced at Ariston.

"She's quiet," Quillan said.

"Uh, yeah," Ariston replied, glancing between the two of us. He and I may have been one step up from strangers, but it was probably pretty clear to him by now that I was anything but quiet.

"Well, let's get going. We're going to escort you back to the interior," Quillan replied, nodding towards the larger force of soldiers. "They'll take care of the forces coming this way."

He looked at us both and then to Drest, Bion, and the handful of others who were bringing up the rear with us.

"I'm Quillan, by the way," he said.

Drest looked at me meaningfully but had the good grace not to say anything.

"Ariston," the other replied, holding his hand out to Quillan.

The men shook each other's hands and nodded in that male bonding sort of way that women never fully understand.

"Come on."

Ariston reached back and grabbed my hand and we were off and running. The mud was sticky and red in the riverbed, yet again something completely new to me. My feet sank into it and it was harder to run with it sucking at my boots. Each time I pulled a foot out, a hole was left behind. I could tell by the tracks left by Quillan and the others that my footprints filled with water not long after my boot was free from the sticky mire.

"Are you okay?" Ariston asked me when he had the chance.

"Yeah," I replied.

"You look like you've seen a ghost."

"I think I have."

"What do you mean?"

We'd made up the distance to Kallisto and the forward group. She looked at me with a relieved expression on her face—nothing had happened to us. We came to a stop right behind her. She and the sergeant were discussing an evacuation plan. She touched him with the familiarity of a friend, but the look in her eyes told me that she wasn't one hundred percent sure that she agreed with his course of action. Quillan walked around the group and joined a comrade of his own.

I glanced at Ariston. I didn't even bother to listen to what Kallisto and the soldier were deciding; I would just follow whatever order came when it was time.

"Quillan," I whispered to Ariston.

"What about him?"

"I know him from—"

"From *before*?"

"Yeah."

"Were you two—?"

"Together?" I asked.

His eyebrows drew together. "Yes."

"No. Not like that."

"Friend?" Ariston guessed.

"A little more than that," I replied, hugging my arms around my chest. "I thought he'd been killed."

Ariston shrugged. "That's a surprise."

"Like you wouldn't believe," I replied.

"Will you tell him who you are?" he asked, glancing up at my unruly hair that I'd kept short and spiky because I liked the look and ease of it. "I'm sure you look different from how he remembered you."

"Not if I can help it," I replied, thinking of my haunting ice-blue eyes.

"Why not?"

"I'm different now," I explained. "He's different. There's something…I don't know. I mean, I thought he was gone. I'd made peace with it."

He nodded, looking perhaps a bit more concerned than he should have been. "The mind does that. It helps you hang on to those things you don't want to forget. Our perception changes things so we remember it easier," he said. "But that's just a theory. I think you should tell him."

I looked over at Quillan, who seemed younger than I remembered. He high-fived a friend of his and he laughed with a lightness that I didn't have any longer. I think it would have been appealing a couple of months before, but now it seemed out of place and completely foreign.

"I'd want to know," Ariston added solemnly.

"Yeah," I grumbled, non-committal.

145

"Especially if I'd been in love with you," he replied before he walked off.

I stared at him in mute incredulity.

Chapter 19

The sun was dipping below the horizon, the mosquitoes had come out for their evening snack, and we could still hear the rumbling of the tanks far off in the distance. Reports continued to come in from the battalion that had stayed behind. They were holding the line. I wondered if the action would be contained or if it would mean war. I wondered if Texas was capable of launching an offensive against an enemy so large.

The kids were getting tired and some of the older members of the group seemed to be slowing down. Kallisto must have noticed the same thing when she looked around because just minutes after she touched the sergeant on the shoulder and whispered something in his ear, we were coming to a stop for the time. Transportation was due within the next thirty minutes and then we'd be on our way out.

"We should be safe here," he said. "Everyone stay together and don't wander off."

I glanced at Drest. He watched me with a fatherly look in his eye. "Are you okay, kiddo?" he asked.

"Yes," I replied, stepping over to him so that we could talk without anyone else hearing.

A picnic site seemed to materialize before us; someone had started a fire. I swatted a mosquito on my arm and watched Ariston try not to watch me.

"I thought you said he was dead," Drest continued gently.

"I thought he was," I confessed with a flabbergasted shrug. "I saw him go down right in front of me."

"What are you going to do?"

"I guess I have to tell him," I replied. "He's going to figure it out eventually."

"You don't want to tell him?" How well Drest knew me.

"Not really. He always wanted us to be more. I loved him as a friend, but never the way I think he always wanted. I think the 'me' of right now really isn't compatible with who he still is." I watched him play-wrestle with one of his fellow soldiers. They took a tumble and then stood to pat each other on the back before going at it again. It seemed like such schoolyard play. The last time I had been in a similar situation, it'd been anything but playful.

Chapter 20

Five Months Ago, or Four Weeks into the Journey

We'd been out for a bit over two months when we came upon a small town where Decima knew everyone's name. It was a chance for a hot shower, a soft bed, and some good food for a few days—a welcome change on the hard journey that wasn't even half over at that point.

Drest and I stuck together like glue, but Decima went to enjoy some quality time with a "friend" of hers. We'd been in the town of Desolation for a day, and despite its name, the town was clean and well-kempt—better even than the settlement in Texas that was probably tank fodder now. We made our way into a pub, the Gilroy, and pulled stools up to the bar.

The alcohol in the South was golden brown but "kicked like a branded horse," as Ben the bartended claimed. He was a short, stout man with balding head and funny little round glasses. He seemed to either have a beer, whiskey, or a woman in his hand at all times. Life was different outside of the Society I was used to—

it was dirtier, but it was also more real than anything I'd ever imagined.

Ben grinned at me as he poured the golden liquor into a shot glass—one for me and one for Drest—and raised his own bottle overhead.

"To your new life!" he exclaimed.

We shot the whiskey that felt like fire burning down my throat. It was the kind of alcohol that was like a swift kick to the chest. Ben drew two long suckles off of the bottle before filling our glasses again and slamming the bottle down.

"Slow down partner," Drest said, holding his hand up. "We need some food if we're going to keep this pace up."

Ben glared at Drest and pointed a finger at him, just inches from his nose. He began wagging the finger in Drest's face. The fat man suddenly burst out into laughter and clapped a hand down on the bar.

"You're absolutely right," he said, gesturing for a girl wearing impossibly short shorts to come to him. "Dottie," he said to the girl, "give them whatever they want. Just put it on Decima's tab like always."

She smiled at the man and looked expectantly at us. "What can I get you?" she asked coyly, eyeing Drest up and down. I wondered if she was offering things off the menu as well.

I ordered something called a hamburger. It seemed like a safe choice: meat, vegetables, bread, something called mayonnaise. Dottie looked at Drest.

"What would you suggest?" he asked. "We're not used to much of this kind of thing."

She slinked over to him and slid her arm around his shoulders. He looked at me questioningly and I raised an eyebrow as I watched her make her play. I took a slow draw off of the top of my whiskey.

"Well, what do you like?" Dottie asked. "We have some good fried chicken. Are you a leg man, or a breast man?" she asked, taking advantage of the proximity to rub said anatomical parts against my friend.

"You know, on second thought," Drest replied, "I'll have what Bryn's having."

Dottie dropped her arm and straightened abruptly. "Oh. Fine," she replied and stalked off.

Drest and I chuckled at her antics until my eye caught sight of another man glaring at us. I watched him over Drest's shoulder. The man viciously played an unfamiliar game at a green topped table with long sticks and balls. He jabbed the sticks at the balls that hit each other with a crashing sound. I wondered if he was going to break them. After each strike, he scowled in our direction.

Drest watched me carefully throughout the rest of our meal—I declined any further whiskey from Ben, much to his disappointment. Drest didn't say anything, though. When we'd finished, we left with as little ceremony as possible. Dottie frowned at our departure, but Ben promised more drinks before we left town. I smiled and thanked him, exchanging another look with the glaring man in the corner before we walked out the door.

The sun had gone down and the air had kicked up, bringing with it a cool humidity and smells I wasn't accustomed to—faint hints of pine and earth.

"Want to take a walk?" Drest asked.

"Sounds great," I replied. I loved being with Drest—we could talk all day long or just sit in companionable silence; each was just as enjoyable as the other.

We strolled past storefronts and another pub, further from the activity of the center of town. Insects hummed in the trees and the stars were emerging above the pine trees.

"Hey!" someone shouted from behind us.

We both turned on a heel and found the glaring, ball-striking man stomping towards us.

"Uh oh," Drest said flatly, without much concern.

"I want to talk to you!" the man yelled at him.

"Alright friend, let's talk."

"Don't call me 'friend,' you son of a—"

"Hey!" I yelled. "There's no need for name calling."

"I think there is, Toots," he replied. "He's messing with my girl."

"What are you talking about?" Drest asked.

"Dottie?" I asked.

"Yeah," the man sniffed.

"Look friend, I don't want anything to do with your girl and I don't want any trouble," Drest replied, raising his hands in surrender.

"I told you not to call me 'friend,'" the man said again and shoved *my* friend in the chest.

Drest fell back onto his rear end and looked at the man in shock. The man lunged for him again and I stepped between them.

"Back off," I said.

"Ooh," the man said, "maybe you want to play." He leered at me in a way only very bad men look at women in a dark place. "I could take you.

"You can try," I replied—sometimes tough talk is enough to scare people away. Not this time.

He tried to tackle me, but I kicked him in the gut. Crumpling into a ball at my feet, he grabbed at my legs to take me down. My training took over and I let him pull me to the ground. He was heavy and stank of stale beer.

I felt my back sink into the soft soil. I twisted under him and he laughed in my face, pushing his pelvis against mine. I rotated my hips so I could slide out from under him.

In a twist that I didn't recall learning, I was suddenly behind him with my legs wrapped around his neck.

At first he grinned as if that was exactly what he'd prefer most in the world, but when I cut his airway off, his face turned red as he flailed about. The way we were positioned, my thighs were around his neck from behind, my back against his, so he couldn't reach around to strike me.

I didn't think, I just moved on trained instinct. He beat his closed fist against my shin and I could tell it was starting to bruise. And then I twisted my hips in one sharp jolt. The man went limp beside me and I scurried out of his reach.

"My God!" Drest murmured. He had pulled himself up off of the ground during my struggle and now he stood over the body of the man.

He reached down and placed two fingers against his neck.

"Is he…?" I asked.

"Yes," he replied. "He's dead."

My heart raced and it was then that the adrenaline finally kicked in. "I've killed a man," I whispered.

"He was going to hurt us," Drest replied.

"I should have been able to take him down without doing that," I said again, staring at the body in the mud.

"You did the right thing," Drest said firmly, "he was going to hurt us."

"I don't know how that happened. I don't even remember learning some of that stuff."

"It's alright."

"I didn't mean to do that."

"Bryn!" Drest said sharply.

I looked up at him in shock.

"He was going to hurt us. If anyone asks me, you had no other choice," he said firmly. "Do you understand?"

I nodded in reply; it was all I could muster.

***

Today, a little girl ran by, brushing up against my leg, and I was suddenly back in the present. I watched Quillan wrap his own legs around his buddy's chest with a burst of laughter. His friend tapped the ground and Quillan jumped up to let him stand.

No, things were definitely different.

Chapter 21

Present Day: Ariston

Ariston sat sharpening his knife and watched Bryn talk to Drest. She talked to him without looking at the older man. They had a curious way with each other. One always knew where the other was, and it was rare for them ever to be very far apart. She looked upset, but she was too far away for him to read her lips well; the haze from the campfire, like a hot oasis, shimmered in the air before his face.

Her eyes darted to Ariston from time to time but didn't linger there. He wanted them to, but if there was something he'd learned from life, it was that you don't always get what you want. Instead Bryn seemed to be preoccupied by the guide Quillan.

Ariston followed her line of sight and watched the other man play-wrestle with his friend. When he pinned the other soldier to the ground, he laughed and they shook hands. Ariston looked back over at Bryn who was still talking to Drest as she frowned at Quillan.

"Hey there," that familiar sultry voice said from behind.

He didn't even have to turn around. "Hey Kallisto," he said. "What's new?"

"Nothing to report," she said. "It looks like we made it out of there with nearly everyone." She sighed as she sat down on the log beside him.

He could tell she was watching him, but he didn't look at her.

"What's on your mind?" she asked, looking from him to Bryn and then back again. "The girl?"

He shook his head, but didn't argue. "She's different."

"Well *yeah* she's different," she said as if it were the most obvious thing in the world, even to a fool. "She's part of the monarchy, part of the big, bad Government. Or—she was. That makes her a different person than the rest of us."

He shook his head. "No," he replied, "I mean she's different in other ways. Sometimes she thinks about things—I mean really considers them, and then at other times, she does something out of the blue, without thinking at all. It's like it's just automatic. She could have run circles around me and Bion on the way in. It was no big deal to her."

Kallisto considered it, watching Bryn carefully. "You think they modified her?" she asked.

He shrugged. "Maybe."

"Shit. That means she's got a—"

"Yeah," he said, standing up abruptly and walking off. He stepped past the fire and past the group of kids that were playing nearby under the wary eye of their parents. If he'd not been focused on other things, he may have felt sympathy for them.

Chapter 22

Bryn

Ariston walked towards me with more purpose than I'd ever seen from him. He had a look in his eyes that had my heart pounding. He stepped over stones and felled branches without looking at his feet. I resisted the urge to step back when he reached me.

"Give me your arm," he said.

I looked at him suspiciously but gave him my right arm.

"The other one."

Without a word, I turned so that he could take my arm in his hands. I watched him as he tapped his index and middle finger against the skin on the inside of my upper arm. He moved around until he felt something just above my elbow where the skin was firmer close to the joint. He cursed under his breath.

"What is it?" I asked.

165

He reached down and grabbed my other hand. He pressed my fingers against a small place on my arm.

"There," he said. "Do you feel that?"

I moved my fingers around, pushing into the soft part of my arm. There was a hard edge of something there, where it should have just been muscle tissue. I looked up at him in shock.

I switched arms and felt around above my right elbow. Nothing. Feeling my left elbow again, my fingers moved around until I could feel a round disc-like implant no bigger than my thumbnail under the skin.

"What the hell is that?" I exclaimed.

"A tracking device," Ariston said.

"What?" Drest and I asked together.

"You've been neurologically modified. The stuff you're able to do—the knowledge you just seem to possess, the actions that seem to be instinctual—that's all been programmed into your brain. And that," he said, jabbing at my arm, "is how they keep track of their little projects."

"My God," Drest said quietly.

At first I couldn't believe it. On the surface it didn't seem possible, but once I started thinking about it all—the guy I'd killed in Desolation, the incident that caused me to lose my sword, my escape from my previous home—the more it started to make sense. My eyes shifted around the campfire as I played with the small disc. My gaze rested on Kallisto who sat staring at us through the heat of the campfire.

I trudged over to her. She continued to watch me. I was walking so fast that the men had to jog to keep up with me—*was that part of my modification process?*

"What are you doing?" Ariston asked.

"Do you have a knife?" I asked Kallisto, ignoring everyone else.

"You can't do that," Drest said, already one step ahead of me.

Kallisto handed me her black combat knife without a word.

"What are you doing?" Ariston asked again.

"Got any alcohol?" I asked Kallisto.

She pulled a flask out of a pack she'd gotten off of her sergeant and handed it to me. She looked at me confidently but still didn't say a word.

I unscrewed the cap and poured some of the amber liquid on my arm. The smell reminded me of the bar in Desolation. I took a swig, recapped it, and handed it back to her.

"Stop that, Bryn," Drest said as I laid the edge of the knife against the skin of my arm.

"Do you want to do it?" I asked briskly—I couldn't afford to let anyone scare me right before I cut into my own body.

He stepped backwards. "No," he replied, holding his hands up.

I glared at Ariston and then back at my arm. I pushed the tip of the blade into my skin and hissed at the pain as bright red blood started to bead up at its point. I panted heavily and blinked tears from my eyes.

"I can't," I whispered, not sure which hurt more, the physical pain or the admission of weakness.

Kallisto's stare shifted between me and Ariston. He silently walked behind me and cradled my left arm with his own. His right hand came down on mine gently and pulled the blade away.

"I'll do it," he whispered gently.

I nodded and leaned against him for support. I wrapped my other arm back around his waist so I wouldn't be tempted to rip the knife from his hand.

"Ready?" he asked.

"Just do it."

I leaned my head against his shoulder and looked up. In the twilight sky I could see the hints of stars emerging from the dusky violet blue.

I stared at these tiny pinpoints of light when a flash of pain struck my arm. I grunted in response and pushed my back against Ariston's chest.

"Shh, shh, shh," he crooned.

I looked down at my arm. He'd cut a slit in my skin so that it looked like a little smile was carved there. He handed the knife to Kallisto. She passed him a piece of gauze from a medical kit that seemed to have magically appeared. He dabbed at the bright blood on my arm.

"Hold your breath," he said softly.

I did as he instructed and watched as he tried to push the disk out from under my skin like he was removing a splinter. I was shiny and seemed so small in comparison to the amount of pain it caused me as he tried to free it.

I groaned and bit my lip, tasting blood.

"That's strange," he said, trying to pull the disc out with a piece of gauze.

The pain shot up my arm and into my shoulder. I cried out in pain.

Ariston immediately let go of the foreign object and I sighed in relief.

"I think it's connected to something further up my arm," I panted.

He and Kallisto exchanged a look as he took another piece of gauze and a bandage from her and wrapped my arm. He pulled my hand towards my shoulder and told me to hold it there. His other arm wrapped around my waist and held me.

"Are you alright?" he asked.

I nodded breathlessly and leaned against him. It's funny how we just want a hug when we hurt.

"We need to get you to Tryphon," he said. "He can get it out or at least make sure everything is deactivated."

I nodded. I didn't care where Tryphon was or how long it would take to get there. I looked at the group of refugees that had assembled in the clearing. The school teacher Ena, the kids—some of whom were yet to be teenagers—and their parents, Texan officials and volunteers alike were all at risk if I didn't act. And the odds were stacked against my survival, but I had to try.

"Tryphon lives near the border for this reason. He can help you; he's made it his life's mission to live in harm's way just to help refugees," Ariston explained anyway, "but we have to skirt a little south to avoid that." He pointed in the direction we'd run from.

"I have to go," I said.

"You can't go alone," Ariston said.

I smiled. "I thought you'd say that."

"I'm going to tell the sergeant. We'll get a team assembled and we'll go together," Kallisto said.

"You're coming with us?" Ariston asked.

She grinned mischievously. "Hell yeah. I wouldn't miss it for the world." She walked off towards her sergeant, slinging her pack over one shoulder.

Chapter 23

"What's the latest from the battalion?" I asked Kallisto as we stood around a map that had been spread out on a large, ragged boulder.

"They're holding the line, but the enemy keeps pushing. Reinforcements are coming up from the south to intercept them," she looked over her shoulder, "but there's the transport for these people. We're going to take a jeep and head this way." She pointed at the map and traced her finger along a line westward.

Kallisto's sergeant leaned over her with a hand on her shoulder. "It'll put you right in the line of fire of the forces at the border."

"I don't have a choice," I said quickly. "They won't stop as long as they can find me." I held my arm up as evidence.

He nodded. "You take a couple of my men along."

It didn't seem like I would have a choice.

He snapped his fingers. "Noe! Smythe!"

I groaned inwardly as Quillan and his wrestling buddy walked over. I tried not to look at Ariston, but my eyes went immediately to Drest. He nodded in sympathy.

"Take a six person jeep and go," the sergeant told Kallisto.

She nodded and signaled to Bion who stood a few yards off. He ran up and she relayed the plan to him. He looked at me with a worried expression, unconsciously rubbing the inside of his own arm, as Kallisto briefed him.

I turned to Drest.

"There's not room for me, kiddo," he said, articulating my thoughts perfectly.

I nodded. "I know."

"It's okay," he said. "I'll be safe and we'll meet again soon. Kallisto and Ariston will know where I end up."

I wanted to protest, but I knew he was right. Instead I jumped into his arms and squeezed him as hard as I could.

"I'll see you soon, girl," he whispered.

I hoped he was right.

Ariston touched me lightly on the shoulder. "We're ready when you are," he said softly.

"Already." I said. It wasn't a question.

Drest released me and smiled. "Go," he said.

"The jeep was already loaded up," Ariston replied softly. "We just have to jump in."

I nodded. "Be safe," I said to Drest as Ariston pulled me toward the jeep.

Drest waved once more as Decima came to stand beside him. Of course. She'd watch out for him.

"'Ello there," the one named Smythe said as we approached. His voice sounded funny; I'd never heard an accent like his before. He shoved his hand out in greeting.

"Come on!" Quillan said from behind the wheel. "We can talk on the ride."

He glanced at us too fast to really look at anyone and turned the key in the ignition. Bion jumped in the back and strapped himself into one of the very back seats. Kallisto took the seat next to him, which left two seats for me and Ariston in the center of the vehicle. Smythe grinned at us as he jumped into the passenger seat moments before Quillan took off.

"Well, you all know this is Smythe," Quillan began, steering the heavy open-air vehicle over the rough terrain. "I'm Quillan."

"I'm Kallisto," she began. "This is Bion, Ariston, and Bryn."

Quillan jerked the wheel to the side at the sound of my name, jolting us all. He looked back at me in the rearview mirror every couple of seconds, narrowing his eyes at me at one point until Smythe caught his attention.

"Oi!" he called. "Watch the path, mate."

"Sorry," he murmured and reluctantly pulled his eyes away from me.

Ariston looked down at me, but he didn't say anything.

"Uh, so Bryn," Quillan began. My heart rate increased. "Where are you from?"

There was no way around it. Might as well come clean. "The New York District," I replied.

"What?!" he exclaimed, slamming on the breaks.

We all lurched forward in our seats. Bion groaned and rubbed his head. Quillan turned around in his seat and stared at me in shock. His eyes moved across my face, up to my hair, down to my feet, until they rested on my ice blue eyes.

"I thought it was you, but you look so different," he said.

Smythe watched him carefully. He glanced at Ariston who sat protectively by my side.

Ariston sighed and looked at Quillan. "Do you want me to drive so you two can catch up?"

"Uh," Quillan said, looking from him to his buddy in the next seat over. "Uh, I'll let Smythe drive."

"Well shove over then, mate."

Quillan jumped out of the jeep and walked around the front. His surprised eyes never left me for a moment. Smythe, on the other hand, slid over to the driver's seat and buckled himself into it.

"What happened?" Quillan asked excitedly once we began moving again.

"What do you mean?" I asked simply. "I thought you were dead and I left—just like we'd planned. I just had to go it alone for a while."

"No," he said, "I mean with your hair and your eyes."

Ariston snickered under his breath. I glanced at him but otherwise didn't comment on his reaction.

"Most of us have had some of our DNA changed," I replied, explaining the process as Drest and I had experienced it. "A supplement changed my hair overnight, and they have the technology to change the structure of your eyes during the course of twenty-four hours or so."

Quillan glanced at Smythe.

"It's true, mate," Smythe shrugged. "I didn't always look like this."

"Wow," Quillan replied. "So how long did it take you to get to Texas?"

"A bit over six months."

"Wow," he said again. "I missed you Bryn."

The air seemed to tighten around us even as the wind whipped over our bodies.

"I know," I replied.

"You know?" he asked, taken aback.

I glanced at the terrain we covered. I turned back and looked him in the eye. "Yeah," I replied. "I know."

"Didn't you miss me?" he demanded.

I sighed and glanced at Ariston. Kallisto remained completely silent, which wasn't unusual for her. Bion just watched me.

"Do we really have to do this now?" I asked.

"Yes, we do. What's wrong with you, Bryn?" he asked, and I could tell that I'd hurt his feelings. "Did you miss me?"

I sighed. "Of course I did, Quillan. I thought you'd died. The memory of those last moments haunted me for months. I've never felt so helpless. You were my best friend. What do you think?"

"I think about you all the time," he said and it sounded like a confession. "When did you forget about me?"

I frowned at him in disappointment. "Don't be stupid. I never forgot about you."

"Then why didn't you say something when you first saw me?"

I exhaled heavily. "For this very reason. Because despite our relationship, I think I've always meant more to you than you have to me." I glanced at Smythe's reflection in the rearview mirror. He was scowling. "And I don't like to be mean."

"Nice work on that," Smythe grumbled.

"Hey," Ariston warned softly and Smythe turned his attention back to the path ahead of the jeep.

Quillan sighed and turned around in his seat to face the windshield. I glanced in Ariston's and Bion's direction. They watched me protectively. I turned away and looked out at the land that we drove over.

***

Quillan and I had played chess at one of the underground clubs that we weren't supposed to be at, one of the clubs that was always threatening to overflow out the door because so many people sneaked away to go. We were still in school, several years ago.

"Check," Quillan had said with a grin across the table. It was then twelfth time we'd played against one another – yes, I'd kept count.

The game had taken over two hours to reach this point and he had no clue that I was ready to beat him in two moves. Our relationship had been built on a foundation of the strategy game. You can learn a great deal about another person playing such a game.

"That's what you think," I said and moved a piece. My king was immediately safe and his was in great danger of getting cornered.

"How about that?" he replied, increasing his response time when things were coming down to the wire. I didn't know it at the time, but I would soon learn that this is how he responded in an emergency—he was impulsive.

"Checkmate."

"No!" he replied, with a confused look on his face. "Can't be."

"Check it," I replied, knowing that my position was iron-clad.

He shook his head and grinned at me. "One of these days, Bryn Craw, I will win against you."

"Until then," I replied with a laugh.

***

Those were the days, I thought as my body was rocked back and forth with the rocking of the jeep as we continued along.

"So what's the deal here, mates?" Smythe asked from behind the steering wheel, his words releasing the tension that seemed to feel the air around us.

"We need to get over to Tryphon so he can get the tracking device out of her arm," Ariston said.

"Tracking device?"

"Yeah," I replied. "They think it is part of the training I received, a way for them to keep track of me while I was being programmed. Now I just can't get away."

"Oi!" Smythe replied. "Programmed? What do you mean by that? I've never heard of that before."

"She knows things that she doesn't remember learning," Ariston replied. "She acts on instinct when it comes to certain things that you can only learn—it's not as if you're born knowing how to kill a man."

I looked at Ariston in shock. I'd never told him I'd killed anyone. "How do you know that?" I whispered.

He smirked at me. "Really?" he asked sarcastically.

"Is that why some days you couldn't tell me what you did all day?" Quillan asked.

I started at the question. Kallisto, Bion, and Ariston turned to look at me. I had never given it much thought, but maybe there was something to his question. There had been so many times that hours and hours would pass during the course of the day and I'd come home exhausted without remembering much of the day. When Quillan asked what I'd done with my day, the explanation was laughably insufficient.

"Probably so," I answered.

"So…how much further do we have to go?" Bion asked.

"Tryphon's outpost is about thirty miles off," Kallisto replied. "Why?"

"Because we've got company," he replied, loading the rifle that lay across his lap.

I turned in my seat and looked in the direction that Bion indicated. Over the berm of green and stone came a force on foot. They saw us as soon as we saw them. They raised their guns.

Smythe hit the brakes. At first, the action didn't make any sense to me, but with a sweep of the eye I realized that we were surrounded. Hitting the gas wouldn't have done anything except get us shot.

We jumped out of the jeep and crouched behind it, peeking around the corners at the force above us.

"Shit," Bion whispered—it was a word that would have gotten him a few days confinement in the world I once knew. Jail was the least of our concerns today.

"What do we do?" Smythe asked.

In a synchronized motion, my friends and I turned to him and gave him a questioning look.

"He's navigation," Quillan grumbled without looking away from the force on the other side of the jeep.

"Identify yourselves!" a male voice called from the armed soldiers.

We exchanged looks silently.

"We just want Guardian Trainee Bryn Craw!"

Kallisto squeezed my arm and gritted her teeth.

"Send her out and the rest of you can go on your way. We want nothing to do with the Republic of Texas," the same man said.

Ariston cocked his rifle and Kallisto did the same.

"That's not possible," Quillan said, staring hard into my eyes. "She's not here."

There was murmuring among the group and the sound of people walking forward. I looked at Bion for an explanation; he had the best view, but he just shook his head at me. I peeked between seams in the jeep's side panel. The force was holding the line.

"*That*," a familiar voice said, "is a lie."

My breath caught in my chest and I would have sworn my heart stopped for a moment. "Damn it!" I whispered.

Bion groaned.

"Who is that?" Ariston whispered to me.

"I can't believe she came all the way out here. I knew she was behind it, but to come out here—what's she trying to prove?" I muttered to myself.

"Bryn?" Ariston asked. "Who is she?"

The familiar voice called out again, taunting me. "Bryn! Oh Bryn!" she sang. "Come out to play!"

"My sister," I replied flatly.

I frowned. I knew it could go either way: I would be able to talk myself out of the situation or I'd have to try to fight my way out. And I couldn't just hide and do nothing—even if I wanted to do. I shifted my weight from one foot to another, as Melisent continued to sing in my direction, her voice becoming shrill.

"Come out to *play-ay*!"

I stood slowly with my hands behind my back—the gun Kallisto had given me was in my right hand and the fingers of my left rested on the Down Stick shoved my back pocket.

"No!" Quillan exclaimed in a whisper.

I silenced him with a look.

"Ah! Bryn, my dear sister, there you are," Melisent crooned, recognizing me only as my sister could, despite my physical changes. "I've come to bring you home."

"That's not going to happen," I replied.

My sister pursed her lips and glared at me. Even from a distance, I could see she let out an angry exhalation of air. She stood in the light blue robes she preferred—they were supposed to symbolize some saintly woman her Society had nearly forgotten. I never understood the significance, but maybe that was because my sister was anything but a saint.

"You could die," Melisent said ambiguously.

"You'd have already killed me if that was the plan," I challenged.

"Ha!" she exclaimed and threw her hands in the air. Her smiled faded. "You're right. I've come to take you home."

"I have no home."

"Damn it all, Bryn!" she shrieked.

Out of the corner of my eye I watched Bion slowly rise to stand beside me.

"She doesn't want to go," he said in a booming voice.

"Silence!" Melisent said.

I glanced down at Smythe who leaned against the jeep near my feet. He was typing furiously at his communication device and glancing up at the air behind us. He realized I was looking at him and he smiled. He silently pointed to his eyes and then up at the sky behind me. He held up three fingers and mouthed the words *three minutes.*

I didn't know what was coming in three minutes, but I hoped to the god Drest always called on that it was the cavalry. I glanced sideways at Bion.

"We need three minutes," I whispered.

"Come home, Bryn," Melisent said again. It was go time.

I deliberately stepped around the jeep, ignoring the silent protests of my friends. I walked slowly behind Bion and came to stand on his other side. Ariston, Quillan, and Kallisto all had their weapons at the ready, covering me as well as they could against a force of thirty or so trained soldiers.

"That's a good girl," my sister said. "Come to me and I won't hurt your friends. We don't want a war."

"No."

I stepped further into the space that spread out between the two groups of people—the free Texan land between the rebels and the power of her Government.

Melisent snapped her fingers and two men rushed me. Before the first could grab my arm, I stepped forward and landed the Down Stick halfway between his hand and his elbow, feeling the bone give way under the force. He cried in pain as he fell to the ground, clutching the limb with his uninjured hand. I swung around and leveled the pistol squarely at the other man's forehead. He froze in his tracks.

"I said: No."

Melisent held her hands up to the rest of her force, holding them back.

I glared at her, my weapons still ready. "You claim you don't want a war."

"Yes."

"And you storm into a free territory with guns blazing."

"To free my sister!" she whined.

"I *AM* FREE!" I yelled across the gully, glaring first at the man at the other end of my pistol, and then at my sister. "You don't want me free. You would take me back to your way of life: a life of lies and a life of oppression. Well sister, I've found another way to live. I've hacked it out of the wilderness and I've devoured the ideals of freedom like I was starving. The Government's a machine of tyranny."

"Don't listen to her, the poor thing's gone crazy," Melisent said in faux-sympathy.

I laughed at her in a way I'd never laughed at her before—and she knew it. I laughed the laugh of the wise woman who knows better, the laugh of the revolutionary who is willing to die for what she believes in. I laughed the laugh of someone who had nothing to lose.

My heart should have raced, tension in every breath, but I was calm as I glanced over my shoulder and saw my friends slowly creep up behind me, guns drawn and aimed at my enemy. If I wasn't born for this, then I was certainly molded for it, shaped probably from infancy. I was made into this.

I had never felt so alive.

Then a man I knew well stepped through the crowd of soldiers. The men and women of their army parted for him to pass. I shook my head in disgust.

"General Bardot," I greeted grimly. "I never thought I'd see you again. I should have known you'd be behind this." I nodded toward my sister.

"Duty calls, Trainee Craw," he grumbled.

"And yet you *could* have said no."

"And miss a chance to bring you in?" He laughed. "Never."

He was tall and towered over my sister. I knew from experience that he was a powerful man, both in word and in physical form. I'd sparred with him on various occasions and he'd left more than his share of bruises on my body. And that was outside of the training arena.

Of course Melisent's army was under his command—she wouldn't have been able to command a force to save her life. She had power, but no control, no sense of responsibility or leadership. It would take someone of Bardot's caliber to breach the borders of the Republic just to come after one person. If I knew him like I thought I did, he wanted to make an example out of me while he was at it.

"What do you get out of it?" I asked, stalling for time.

"Fame," he replied with an arrogant shrug. "Probably a medal. A pat on the back from your dear old daddy."

"He's not my 'daddy,'" I interrupted with a snort.

The general grinned maniacally. "Well, whatever you call him. I bet he'll give me a promotion."

"Advisor to the Regina?" I asked sarcastically.

Bardot glanced at my sister and turned his head to the side when he looked back at me. "Perhaps."

"Fine," Melisent interrupted—the attention had strayed too far from her for too long. "You want to talk about this, we'll talk about it."

"We are talking about it," I replied, glancing at Smythe. He held up one finger.

"Oh Bryn!" Melisent yelled, exasperated. "You *know* what I *mean*!"

"God you can be shrill," I replied with a sigh. "Alright, I go first. Why do you want me back so badly?" I glanced at Bardot when I asked it and then turned my attention to my sister.

Melisent looked away from me, hesitating.

"It's not like you missed my company," I prodded.

She rolled her eyes.

I could practically feel the tension rolling off of my friends who now gathered around me, their guns pointed defensively in various directions. Our small band of rebels was calmer than the army that stood over us—*they* were used to passivity and we were giving them the exact opposite. The man I still held at gunpoint didn't move a muscle.

"Come on," I said. "I think I know why, but I want to hear it."

Melisent huffed. "Oh alright! I promised Mommy and Daddy I would."

I shook my head. "Why they picked you as successor, I'll never understand. You're nothing but a puppet—" I laughed as realization hit. "My God! That's it, isn't it?"

"What?" she asked, looking around at her forces.

"*That's* why they picked you. They can get anything they want from you." I chuckled and shook my head. "No, Melisent, I'm not going anywhere. You can't make me do anything."

"But *I* can make you," Bardot said.

"Why would you?" I asked.

He looked down on us with a sneer. "Because I hate everything this Godforsaken state is all about. This dirty, stinking place, with its lack of order. How does anything function?" He asked with a sniff of disgust. "It should be wiped from the face of the earth."

Bion nervously shifted next to me.

"It's okay," I whispered to him before addressing Bardot. "I'd advise against starting a war, General. These men and women are more than willing to hack a living out here just to enjoy the full extent of their free will. Sacrifice is nothing compared to the freedom they love. You threaten that, and even I don't know what they're willing to do."

Melisent scowled at me like she did every time someone denied her what she really wanted, any time she didn't get her way. "We'll always find you," she said in an eerily monotonous voice.

"No," I replied, grinning at the sound of helicopters behind me. "No, you won't."

We felt the aircraft before we saw it. The air pounded down on us with each revolution of the blades.

"Get down!" Bion yelled as they flew overhead.

Melisent's forces on the ridge opened fire on the helicopters at Bardot's command, and we ran for cover. A handful of men shielded her from our return fire. The general grinned maniacally at me.

The bootlegged war films I had seen always presented a firefight as something deliberate, like time slowed down as the bullets flew. That's not how it was at all. It was hot and it was hard to see. The helicopters blew dust up from off the ground under the force of their blades. Texan troops came over the ridge under the aircraft and launched grenades at Melisent's forces.

I didn't feel, I didn't think. I tapped into another part of myself— the part that was trained to kill.

I pulled back on the trigger of my pistol and felt the mechanisms within the weapon as the firing pin hit the bullet. The pistol recoiled against the palm of my hand. I could see the bullet as it left the gun and the next thing I saw was the man who fell before me. He certainly wasn't the first man I'd killed, but he was the first I'd killed so impersonally.

Melisent's forces were scattered and they didn't even bother to try to recover their dead. The whole is paramount to the individual—unless that individual was special. They protected Melisent in a way they wouldn't have covered their own mothers. I was sure she'd gotten away.

Kallisto and Bion ran toward the fighting. Bardot hit Kallisto in the shoulder with the butt of his rifle. It turned her body, so she elbowed him in the ribs. Predictably, he dropped this rifle with a demonic smile and reached back to deliver a punch to her left eye. She ducked out of the way so that his fist didn't connect with her cheek. She turned on a heel and pulled the pistol out of his hip holster. Without hesitation, she aimed the gun at the side of his head and pulled the trigger. He collapsed at her feet.

She glanced at me just as I had run out of bullets—fifteen bullets for fifteen enemies. She started to pull her lips into a smile right before a look of shock captured her eyes. Her mouth fell open. She collapsed on the ground in an undignified heap.

"No!" I yelled and started running.

"Stop it!" Ariston said, standing in my way. He wrapped his arms around my waist and held me back.

I twisted against him and tried to fight him off.

"The helicopters," he reminded me.

"Damn it!" I said, tears entering my eyes. "She didn't deserve that."

"No, she didn't," he said in my ear and rocked me a little bit.

The dry brush on the ridge caught fire after the helicopters launched rockets at the enemy, scorching the earth. When it was surreally quiet again, the field was smoldering and smoky; the air, choking. It was over before it even really started.

I hugged Ariston close as I cried. I looked over his shoulder at Quillan, who stood watching us with a look that told me he finally understood how things were. His face was streaked with soot from the fire and he sighed in exhaustion.

"Where's Kallisto?" Bion asked.

Ariston looked at me and then back at him. He nodded toward the ridge that now smoldered.

A similar look of understanding passed over Bion's face, but his wasn't of heartbreak. Bion silently watched the fire burn over his fallen comrade.

"Now what?" I sniffed.

Bion turned to me with a resigned look on his face. "How do you feel about a revolution?"

Chapter 24

Later that Night

"Tell me more," I said while lying on Tryphon's "operating table" that evening. I was lightly sedated with some herb that the old man grew in his garden.

Ariston stood at my head, a hand lightly rubbing my hair in an attempt to comfort me. I didn't look at him. I looked at Bion. But that wasn't his real name.

"I didn't like it anymore," Bion said.

It was hard for me to grasp the concept that the man standing on the other side of the table as the old medicine man started cutting a long line from my shoulder to my elbow was my long-lost brother, Pax. I smiled at him.

"So you left," I said, slurring the words a bit.

"Just like you," he grinned. "I always knew you had spunk."

I smiled and closed my eyes. The room felt like it was spinning. I could feel Tryphon moving tissue out of the way, finding the long anchor line that ran up my arm.

"Why did you—" I struggled to ask "—change? Your name," I breathed. "Why Bion?"

He chuckled. "Try to relax, sis," he replied, squeezing my free hand and glancing at Ariston.

"I will," I grunted against the sedative. "Just…tell me. I will," I promised.

"I read it somewhere and I liked it." He shrugged. "It means life and it seemed to make sense."

I think I smiled.

Chapter 25

Ariston

Bryn seemed helpless as the old man carved into her arm. Ariston watched him warily.

"Do not worry," Tryphon said, his long white beard—which matched his unruly, long white hair—moved when he talked. "She is not in pain."

Ariston nodded and glanced at Bion who stood over his sister. "What are you thinking?" he asked.

Bion rocked back on a heel and looked at his friend. "Let's change the world."

"What's the plan?"

"Head north as soon as she's better," Bion said, nodding towards his sister. "With her on our side, we can finally make this work.

She can get me on the inside and I can take it from there," he replied before turning and walking out of the small hut.

Tryphon ambled around the room, dressed in the greying robes of a hermit. The old man laughed to himself from time to time, which didn't reassure Ariston, but Bryn sighed in her sleep. That made him feel better.

He looked out the window at Bion said something to Quillan and Smythe before walking to the summit of the cliff nearby.

Bion stood with his hand on his hips and looked out at the sunset. He thought about his sister and he thought about the future. And he smiled.

About the Author

Megan Winkler is the author of *Transmissions from Dating Land*, *Wake of Darkness*, and co-author of *Ruins of North Texas* with her partner, Mike Winkler. She holds a Master of Arts in military and American history from American Military University. She lives in North Texas.

www.ingramcontent.com/pod-product-compliance
Lightning Source LLC
Chambersburg PA
CBHW070832120626
46556CB00002B/727